WHAT HAPPENS IN VEGAS

WHAT HAPPENS IN...

TARRAH ANDERS

Book Formatting: Tarrah Anders, LLC

Cover: Sinful Book Hoarder

Ordering Information: What Happens in Vegas

ASIN: B087L9NZ97 | ISBN: 9798644312184

Sometimes, a night in Vegas will change your life.

PROLOGUE

"I PROMISE to ride you like the unicorn that you are, until our dying day," I say looking up at the gorgeous man standing in a tuxedo in front of me. I push up the tiara that was placed on my head and grin.

"And I promise to brush your hair at night, every night." He returns bopping me on the tip of my nose.

I hiccup and giggle like a school-girl as I teeter back and forth on my feet from the slight motion.

I lean up on my tiptoes and we kiss, annoying Elvis standing in front of us for the millionth time since our ceremony began, since every few moments we lean into one another and interrupt what should be a ten-minute ceremony. It's been thirty minutes, and despite there are two Elvis's talking, I can see slight irritation.

"You two will have plenty of time to smooch, but dare I say that I get you two jailbirds hitched?" Elvis says with a roll of his eyes. "Do you two have any more vows that you would like to say to one another?"

"Yes," the gorgeous man in front of me says to Elvis and then returns his glazed gaze to me. "I promise to make sure that you have your endless supply of calendars, so that way you never miss a thing, or an important date," he smiles proudly.

A collective '*Aww*' from the peanut gallery behind us draws my attention away from my husband to be for a split second.

He's dashing, he looks like he knows what he's doing in all the ways that would matter, and those ways would be the bedroom, at least that's all I'm thinking right now.

And while I may be seeing double right now, I can definitely tell that he's a looker.

"Oh, you listened," I gush.

I lean up and kiss him chastely on the lips and pull back when I hear the clearing of the throat.

"Alright, Ms. Peyton, do you take this hunka-hunka burning love to be yours?"

"Sure as fuck, I do." I throw my free hand in the air and pump it. Which encourages more hoots and hollers from our witnesses.

Elvis turns to my handsome groom who is swaying on his own two feet, with a large smile on his face.

"And, Mr. Max, do you take this lady to be your forever Rockabilly princess?"

"Totally do," Mr. Max nods his head.

"And by the power invested in me by the city of Las Vegas and Graceland, I now pronounce you husband and wife, nuhuh-uh-huh!" Elvis does a little shimmy of his hips and his arms spread out in the air. "You may now finally pucker up."

I lean in and nearly fall into Mr. Max, when we kiss and seal our marriage.

Cheers from the peanut gallery erupt as the kiss turns into a fit of giggles.

CHAPTER ONE

"This one time in Vegas, I had drinks with Elvis, RuPaul, Tina Turner and Elton John..."

PEYTON

If I open my eyes, that means the brightness of the room will burn my retinas and I will be blind. I can't afford to be blind. It sounds expensive, and frankly, I don't have the extra money to blind-proof my apartment. I roll onto my back and brush my hair out of my face. The motion itself rattles my head and is painful, so much so, that I want to sink deeper into the mattress. But even that sounds like too much work, and I really don't have the energy. I wrap my arms around my body and touch a whole lot of skin.

Am I naked?

Why am I naked?

I take a deep breath and slowly open my eyes, scan the room

and note that this is not my room. I move onto my side and look to the side of the bed, where I expect to see the other bed with my roommate passed out in it. Except, that's far from what I see. The floor is a different color, with fancy patterns and not of multi-colored 'let's hide any stains', type of carpet that my room has. This floor is clean and has much more space than mine, and based on the floor to ceiling windows' view, is a much better one, whereas the view from the front window of our room is another small hotel. Everything is different.

I slowly push myself to sit up in the bed and note the bed that I'm in is surrounded by windows.

Where am I?

Again, why am I naked?

I pull up the covers and my fingers graze over something on my hand. I pause hoping that it's not what I think it is and I look down as my heart skips a beat and my mouth goes dry.

There is a silver band with a large single diamond on my ring finger sparkling at me. I hold my hand up and turn it, then look at the object weighting my finger again. *This can't be.*

What the ever-loving hell happened last night?

I look beside me as if in slow-motion and that's when I see him.

Who is he? Is this his room? What the hell happened?

A man sleeps, with his back to me. His dark brown hair is disheveled from sleep and I'm pretty sure that he's just as naked as I am.

I can't see any defining features of him, but he doesn't have a hairy back, and it looks like he's got a strong back. The muscles move as he breathes, and I can tell that as I lower my eyes to the lower half of his back, that he's not wearing any clothing either.

Well, that's a win for me, that I didn't hook up with a hairy dude. I could have chosen a beast of a man, but from the looks of him, he's not part animal and part man. But seriously, who is he and was whatever we did last night good?

Another bonus is that this room is fantastic, and this bed is so nice that I almost don't want to get out.

But whatever happened last night and whatever *this* is... cannot be.

I cannot be married to a complete stranger.

In fear of waking the slumbering stranger beside me, I slink out of the soft sheets and tiptoe across the room. I see the white-lace dress that I wore last night on the floor, with my panties and both of my heels.

As quiet as can be, I look around the room. It's a very nice room.

I wish that I could remember last night, but the last thing I remember was my friends telling me that I wouldn't talk to the attractive man in the tux. I remember dancing with him, drinking with him, and then riding in a limo, just the two of us. This must be the guy.

I look over to the bed, where he's sleeping.

If I remember correctly, he is extremely attractive. He has chiseled features, with bright turquoise eyes and a devilish smile. The tux that he wore last night, wore him, he didn't wear it. He filled it out perfectly and even though I wondered why he was wearing a tux, when all his friends weren't, he looked to be comfortable in his skin enough to not give a crap.

A chill runs through my body at a memory of the night. Kissing on the dance floor and his strong hands holding me against him. I shake my head, spot my clutch on a table, grab it quietly to not wake the slumbering man in the bed, then turn to leave the room.

With one last glance back to him, taking in the scene and wondering about what the hell happened last night, I slowly turn the knob and exit.

Walking down the long hotel hallway, I make my way to the elevator Once inside, I take a deep breath and lean my head back against the wall.

Where usually the walk of shame would be an embarrassing thing, in Vegas—you wouldn't know whether or not the person walking down the street had spent the night in the arms of another, playing the slots, or dancing all night long. I move across the lobby in last nights' dress and out to the sidewalk of the hotel.

I open my clutch and sigh heavily when I remember that my cell phone is dead and instead I walk up to the check-in counter, I ask if I can get a cab and soon I am on my way back to the hotel room that I'm sharing with my girlfriends off of the main strip and far from where I am standing.

I take my key out of my handbag and enter in the room, ready for a barrage of questions and loaded with my own as well.

Quinn, my roommate is sitting on the chair in the corner of the room. She has her phone in one hand and coffee in the other.

"About damn time you showed up, what the heck happened to you last night?" she asks loudly, waking up Hanna who bolts up in the bed we were previously sharing.

"That's the same damn question that I have but as you can tell, I was out all night. I think you should pay up now, I went through with talking to the super-hot guy, I think I actually did more than talk to him though."

"I'd say. Last night, it was like you were under some spell, you two were in your own little world. Not us or his friends could separate you guys," she laughs.

"So, you guys hooked up?" Hanna sits up in the bed asking.

I laugh awkwardly, avoiding their gazes while I remove my heels then dig through my suitcase to change into a tank top and shorts and cast aside the dress which promptly landed me a husband.

"Well, Pey?" Hanna pushes, leaning forward and laying on her stomach with her chin fitted in her palm.

"We totally hooked up and I'm sure it was wonderful. If only I could remember any of it," I say pushing my hair off my forehead and out of my eyes.

"Wait a second!" Quinn sets her coffee cup down on the table beside her, stands then rushes to me and grabs my hand. "Shut the fucking front door, what the fuck is that?"

She's staring down at the rock on my ring finger. I pull my hand behind my back, out of sight and try to twist the band off of my finger, but I'm too slow.

Fuck! I forgot to take it off!

"What? What is it? Let me see?" Hanna stumbles out of bed and gets tangled in the blankets. Before almost falling flat on her face, she regains her balance, then makes her way to stand with Quinn staring at the large rock casting a shadow on my hand.

"Did you get married?" Quinn asks standing back to give me the once over as if the ring that she saw on my finger changed the way that I looked.

"I honestly couldn't tell you," I offer casting a glance toward the floor.

"What do you mean?" Quinn places her hand on her hip.

"I mean that I don't remember what happened after a point in the night, then I woke up, and now I'm here." I lift my shoulders and offer her a small smile.

I twist the ring off of my finger and look at it. It's not a fake ring, by any means. It has a good weight to it, and when the light hits it, a prism of colors cascade along the wall. I pocket the ring for now, and make a mental note to figure out what to do with it later.

"And you guys hooked up? I mean obviously, you spent the night with him and your hair looks like a rat slept in it. You totally have *fuck me* hair." Quinn says with a smirk.

"Well, I'm pretty damn sure that he wrecked my vagina because I'm typically not this sore without a little—or should I say a whole lot of action." I say in a sigh.

"Like wrecked as in an hour at spin class or like he sexed you up all night?" Hanna giggles.

"Well, my head feels like I've been in an accident and my lady bits feels like they took a good pounding."

Quinn nods her head in understanding, "So like Rhonda Rousey style, that's awesome. It's been awhile since I've been slammed like that."

I run my hand over my forehead and take a deep breath.

"What do I do? I mean I'm supposedly married to some random guy, where the hell were you guys last night? How did I end up alone with him, I could have been killed!" I look between my two friends as I sit on the edge of the bed.

"Well, you were the one who kind of ditched us. We went to go get drinks and you insisted to stay sitting on his lap, then when we returned, all of you guys were gone."

"That doesn't sound like me," I shake my head.

"We tried calling you a billion times, but it went straight to voicemail. We always tell you that you need to have a full charge if we go out, and yet you never listen." Hanna shakes her head, crossing her arms over her chest, pointing out to me a common occurrence for when we go places.

"So, what do I do now? I'm married, to a complete stranger." I throw myself back on the bed in frustration.

"Well, you know how the saying goes," Quinn starts.

I lean up on my elbows and look at her with a sigh. "What saying?" I ask.

"What happens in Vegas, stays in Vegas!" Quinn and Hanna say in unison.

. . .

MAXWELL

My brain is rattling in my head. My body hurts and I feel like something shit in my mouth.

It's been quite a while since I've let loose like that. But once the guys and I had a few drinks under our belt, I rolled up my sleeves, unbuttoned the top button of my dress-shirt, and untied my bow-tie.

I drank too much and don't really remember getting back to my room. I have very faint memories of last night. I faintly remember making-out with a woman, and that same woman riding in the back of our limo, and her here in bed with me. But there was no woman here in bed with me when I woke up and no signs of a woman being here that I wonder if part of these so-called memories are a dream, or if I really spent the night with some mystery woman.

If it wasn't for the constant chirping from my phone in my pants pocket from the floor, I would have missed my plane.

Begrudgingly, I have an Uber pick me up and drop me off at the airport quickly as I'm moving through the motions, I get to my gate just as they're boarding my group number.

I scan my ticket and head down the boarding bridge.

All I want to do is fall back asleep, which I plan to do once my ass gets into a seat. I take the first available seat that I can find, which is a fucking middle seat and I'm silently cursing my assistant for not booking me a flight with first class seating.

I lean my head back against the seat and then close my eyes.

Once we're in the skies, I recline as soon as allowed and that's the last I remember before landing in Los Angeles.

"THANK YOU FOR AGREEING TO MEET WITH US ON A SUNDAY, MR. Addison," the senior associate of Bean, MacMilliam and Singer leans forward to shake my hand in the lobby of their building.

I offer him a weak smile and pull off my shades.

"My pleasure, I was traveling and thought that this was a perfect detour on the way home, so, how can I be of assistance?" I ask.

"I believe the partners will have all the details. This project wouldn't be one of my case files. I'll be bringing you up to the conference room and you will have all the information there," he explains.

Wordlessly, we ride the elevator up to another floor and he guides me down a long hallway to a glass room where there are four gentlemen sitting at one end of a large rectangular table. The men stand up and eagerly wait for my approach with their hands poised for me to take it in mine. I shake their hands and introductions are made promptly before sitting.

"Thank you for consulting on this merger with us. We have heard amazing things about what you can do and have done for other companies and we hope that you are able to assist us in the same manner."

I thrive on the high of taking two companies and making them one. I've had plenty of experience in the field of finance and business that I've had success rates that no one in the Pacific Northwest has been able to top. Business and gambling are one and the same to me.

When I'm looking for a new venture to take on, I look at what I can do to maximize whatever wealth potential I can get out of a business that makes the rolling of the two companies together easy.

I review the documents and provide my professional opinion in detail over the next few hours before I'm back at the airport and heading home to Seattle.

I walk into my condo with views to die for of the Great Wheel and Elliot Bay. The sky is a mixture of pastels as the lights turn on while walking through the space.

My penthouse is half of the floor, the other half of this floor is shared by one of the other partners at Addison and Drake. At a young age, I've worked hard for this view and I love coming home each and every time to bask in it.

The clicking of nails echoes through the living room as Scout, my best-friend rounds the corner. I've had Scout since I graduated from undergrad. He was a gift from my little sister, and I would be a horrible human if I didn't accept him as a pup. He has kept me company through the years and has created a good bond between my sister and I.

I bend to my knees as the mutt slobbers all over half of my face and laugh as his paws push me onto my back while I rub behind his ears.

"Hey buddy, I've missed you." I say in between moments of Scout's excitement to see me.

I push myself off the floor and with Scout on my heel, walk over to my home office.

After starting my laptop, I sit down at my desk and lean back in my chair.

What a whirlwind of a weekend.

My college best friend is getting married and like a rookie, I don't remember the last twenty-four hours. I've been to Las Vegas many times, and this is the first time in several years that I lost control of who I am. I feel like I did something monumental, but I just can't put my finger on it.

I rack my brain for memories of what happened last night, what happened with the mystery woman.

Who was she? Was she real or a figment of my imagination?

I've got this weird feeling that if she is real that we did more than dance.

CHAPTER TWO

"This one time in Vegas, I woke up outside my room. Had to traipse down to the front desk in pjs and barefoot to get a new key."

PEYTON

The flight back home was obnoxious.

None of the pain pills that I took helped, so my hangover came back from Vegas with me, and there was this guy in front of me snoring so loud and reclined that it took every bit of patience that I had to tune him out. I may have passive-aggressively kicked his seat a few times, but none of the movement made his snoring any quieter.

Pshh. What happens in Vegas definitely didn't stay in Vegas.

Ugh, blasted hangovers crossing state lines.

As soon as the seatbelt noise dings, I get out of my seat

quickly and make it to the front of the plane as they open the doors, and immediately claim a seat.

I'm sitting down with my head in my hands as Quinn and Hanna emerge a few moments later.

"Hey, are you doing okay?" Hanna asks placing her hand on my shoulder with concern.

"I just want to get home and crawl into bed, this headache isn't going away." I explain.

"Oh no, still?" Quinn sits down beside me rubbing my back.

I turn my head to look at her and offer her a small smile.

"Let's get out of here and make sure you get tucked into your bed, and maybe get you a gallon of water, you just need to get all that booze out of you." Quinn stands and offers me her hand. "And definitely, something greasy."

SLOWLY, MY BODY WAKES UP, AND I'M HOME—FACE-DOWN ON my pillow with a puddle of drool underneath me. I push myself up and then wipe the wetness from my cheek. I'm lethargic and feel like Vegas kicked my ass properly.

Now to figure out, what the heck do I do about this damn marriage?

Do Vegas weddings count as real weddings? Especially if one doesn't remember it? Even though, we likely celebrated the marriage?

I mean, I don't think we shared phone numbers, otherwise I'm sure he would have called me by now, right?

Who was he?

Does he remember the night?

And seriously what happened last night?

I swing my legs out of bed, plant my feet on the floor and pull my hair up into a pony tail before making my way to the kitchen.

I dig into the fridge and pull out a bottle of ginger ale that I have hiding in the back and open it.

"Feeling any better?" Quinn bounces into the kitchen while I'm taking a long sip.

I shake my head slightly to see if the headache is still there. "I think I'm good now." I say with a smile.

"Good. So, tell me about your husband, what's he like?" she crosses her arms over her chest and leans her shoulder on the fridge with a smirk and a roll of my eyes.

"I wish I could tell you, but last night is a blur and I am kind of fuzzy on the details. All I know is that I woke up next to him." I reply.

"Do you remember what he looks like?" she questions.

"He was hot, that I remember kind of."

"Well, I may have been two sheets to the wind, but I do remember the whole group of guys were pretty damn hot. I think one of them was getting married or something, so he was taken, but I don't remember which guy that was."

I nod, as if I can picture the group of guys.

I can't.

But I don't want to look like a complete fool and a lush. It's been awhile since I've blacked out.

"Hey, what was I drinking that night?" I ask.

"Well, there was a lot of vodka on their table, you know in fancy ice buckets." Quinn says nodding.

"So, we were in the VIP area?" I further question.

Quinn looks up to the ceiling as if she is remembering the night with her finger on her chin.

"I believe so. When Hanna and I went to the little girls' room and to get more drinks, we couldn't get past the big security guy, because you all had left."

"I can't believe that I had been so stupid," I shake my head.

"Listen, nothing bad happened, you were safe, and even

though you were with strangers, you only managed to get married and nothing else." She laughs.

"Yeah, married. Ugh, my mother would be so proud." I roll my eyes.

"So, you don't remember the sex, like at all?"

"Not one bit." I say shaking my head wishing that out of everything any sort of glimmer of what the night entailed could especially help out.

"Man, I would have climbed him like a tree, he was totally easy on the eyes and looked like a good time," Quinn laughs while fanning herself.

"Either way, to me the night never happened, so that would also mean that I'm not married, right?" I straighten and ask.

"I don't think that's how it works," she shakes her head.

"Well then, what the heck do I do?"

"An annulment?"

"I don't even know who he is, how would that work. Have you checked your phone at all? Did you guys take any photos?"

"I didn't even think of that? Go check your phone too, maybe you got some before your phone died." Quinn says excitedly grabbing her phone from the counter.

I think a moment then dash to my room. I rummage through my purse and dig inside as I fish out my phone.

With shaking hands, I press on the gallery icon and my breath stills. Spinning and sitting on the edge of the bed, I stare at the images.

"Quinn!" I shout.

I hear her as she makes her way from the kitchen to my bedroom. She stands in the doorway with her eyes wide.

"Jesus woman! I thought something bad had happened."

"I think we're going to find out who my husband is," I hold up the phone and say with a weak smile.

She moves beside me with her knee bouncing in anticipation.

"We need to reverse image this. Let's get stalkery on your husband!"

We walk back into the kitchen on a mission and turn on the laptop. She taps on the keyboard and then peers at the screen while chewing on her fingernail. I lean over to see what she's looking at so intently.

Maxwell Addison

Sounds like a fancy name.

I look to Quinn and she shrugs.

"Well, he's not a famous movie star," she says getting up to let me take her place.

I'm scrolling the screen then stop and sit back to let out a breath.

"Do you think? Is that him?" I look to her.

She reaches around me and clicks on a profile photo.

The screens shows a handsome man, in his mid-to-late thirties with a smirk on his face that says; '*I know that I'm good-looking*'. He has a light dusting of facial hair and brown eyes that look like he's up to something. In his profile photo, he's wearing all black with a gray background, the image looks like it's a headshot, but I can't be too certain.

I take control of the track pad and scroll down his profile and there's not much that he's posted. There's a few reposts of some articles, some general posts that it looks like he's made, but nothing that leads to any insight into who he really is.

I open another tab and type his name into the spacebar.

"Holy shit, he has a wiki page."

"Why would he have a wiki page?" Quinn asks.

She clicks on it and the page loads. "Who knows. Anyone can create one. Maybe he thinks he's top shit and made his own. It says he's partner at a law firm and that he's one of the top producing partners, better than his father. Whatever that means. He has a lot—wow, that's a lot of zeroes—of money."

She scrolls down the page even more and I think that both of our eyes widen at the same time when we see the dollar amount of his net worth.

"I still don't understand why he has a wiki page."

"He must know people," she says.

MAXWELL

If there's one thing that I hate about my job, it's billing.

We bill in 6-minute increments and it's so fucking frustrating, since I hate the paperwork portion of my job. I want to be doing things, not recording them. Isn't that what an assistant is for?

When my father passed away last year, in his will and his recommendation to the board, was that I was named partner in the firm with his absence. After all, my last name is on the signage of the business and all the stationary. The board voted and approved the request on a probationary period, which I surpassed their expectations within the second quarter.

I have worked my ass off and have brought in several deals that have put this firm on the map and allowed us to open up a fourth office later this year.

I'm staring at my log for the month and all the numbers on the spreadsheet are blending together. Thankfully, a knock at my door distracts me.

"Yo! Maxi-pad! I brought lunch," my best friend, Jason says grinning holding up a white bag while barging into the office, filling the space with the aroma of food. My stomach growls and my mouth begins to water.

"What did you bring me?" I ask pushing back in my chair and stretching.

"Meat. Delicious meat that will melt in your mouth and make you pray to the cows!"

"What the hell are you talking about?" I ask standing removing my suit jacket, draping it over the back of my chair and rolling up my sleeves.

It's been a week since being back home from Vegas and I'm still racking my brain about the trip. I have been working on a new client to bring my numbers up even more for the year, so I have been practically living at the office. I pulled out a sizeable sum of money for the trip, pulled out triple of what I went to Vegas with on Saturday night and I came back with nothing more than a hangover.

I'm struggling with how I spent so much money, not that I don't have the money to spend, but I am generally better at spending. *What did I do in Vegas?*

"So, have you found her?" Jason asks me.

"Huh?"

"The chick that you hooked up with in Vegas?" He clarifies.

"Was I supposed to be looking for her?" I look at him.

He shoves my lunch in front of me and I begin unwrapping it.

"Dude. It's a cheeseburger." I say with disgust.

"Yeah, what of it? It's supposed to be the best in town," he tells me before taking a bite out of his own.

"I don't like cheeseburgers," I remind him.

"What? That's not a thing." He shakes his head.

"I've never liked cheeseburgers."

"That's bullshit, you're joking, right? Everybody likes cheeseburgers!"

"I like cheese and I like burgers, but I do not like them together."

"I don't understand you," he shakes his head.

"It's not rocket science, and it's always been this way. I've known you for what … fifteen years, and seriously you can't remember that one tiny detail? After all the meals that we've eaten together?"

"I never order your damn shit man, why the hell do I need to keep tabs on your likes and dislikes? I'm not dating you." He shakes his head.

"You would be so fucking lucky," I say using a French fry to drag the cheese off the patty. It does smell good, but I'm not about to jeopardize my taste to eat something as rank as melted cheese mixing with the beef. Cheese doesn't belong on meat, just like pineapples do not belong on pizza, or forks in power outlets. It's not hard to remember and it's not hard to understand.

Once I'm satisfied, I take my first bite and my eyes roll into the back of my head in pleasure.

This is immaculate. The beef is so juicy and there's something smokey yet, sweet about it that I cannot quite figure out.

"You're right, this is some good meat," I tell him just as he takes his final bite.

"So, back to the mystery girl. You guys took off right after we left the club, then you went off in the opposite direction from us, and took the limo. We had to call a car and figure out where the hell our hotel was since you took our driver who knew all the things we needed to know."

"Yeah, man I have no clue where we went or what happened. I could have sworn that we spent the entire night together. I think there was more to that night, but I'm not entirely sure."

"From what I remember, she was hot as hell. Her friends weren't half bad either."

"I wish I could remember." I say shaking my head.

We finish the rest of our lunch, shoot the shit for a little bit then he leaves, and I get back to work while he leaves me alone with the thoughts that I've been avoiding by staying late and busy at work.

Something is irking me about the whole Vegas trip and I'm not completely sure that I'm okay with it.

I TOSS THE SHOT DOWN MY THROAT AND MY FINGERS GRAB another, poised and ready to take that one as well. But I'm waiting for the rest of the guys to catch up.

It's Marcus's wedding day and the guys and I are doing what we do best.

Pre-celebrating the event.

"I think this should be the last shot that we take, you know, because I've got to get up there and say those special words," Marcus says with a slight slur. He doesn't have a very high tolerance.

"Just one more," Jason says holding up his shot.

We all follow suit and after a count of three, take our shot and slam the shot glass down on the table.

"This is the last day of the rest of your life, you're getting married, the first and probably only one of us to do so. We're just saying our goodbyes." Jason says. "Plus, your lady doesn't have a hot bridesmaid, what the fuck is up with that? I need these shots to be able to get through this wedding, since I certainly won't be hooking up."

"Why do you have to be such a sleezeball?" Devin asks.

"Hey, today is the first day of the rest of my life," Marcus smiles proudly correcting him.

"You do have yourself a nice one," I tell him, patting him on the back as Marcus puts his arm around my shoulder.

"You hear that fellas, that right there is why Maxi-pad is my best man." He points at me, as none of the guys are paying attention.

"Thanks man," I reply.

At the end of the night, after the dancing was done and the bar closed up along with the new bride and groom gone, the guys and I sit around a table. Our jackets are off, our ties are undone, and we're completely drunk. We're playing a game of poker, poorly and I'm pretty sure that Cooper has pissed his pants as he's passed out in the chair beside me with the smell wafting in the air.

"I can't freaking believe that Marcus got hitched today, I mean who saw that coming?" Jason slurs taping on the table after throwing down a card.

"Well, they have been together for about a million years," I tell them.

"That's a good point, I mean what is the point of being with someone in a relationship, if you're not testing them out for marriage." Jason replies. "That's why I stay single."

"Right." I nod.

"Regardless, if you can't stay single, you can't mingle. If you know what I mean." Devin places two cards down and pulls more from the pile.

"I think your kind of mingling might mean something different from ours, brother." Jason swings his head as Devin rolls his eyes.

"I mean, how long do you need to be with someone though, to know if you're willing to be tied down to them forever?" Grayson asks lighting up a cigar.

"Dude, my parents got married after two weeks of knowing one another, and like forty years later, they're still bat shit crazy for one another." Jason says nonchalantly. "It's kind of gross."

"I think it depends on the circumstances," I say.

"And what are those circumstances?" Jason's head perks up. "Prey-tell, oh wise-one?"

"Luck. Chemistry. Attraction, hell I don't know. But I do know, that when I find it, I'll be a goner just like Marcus."

"You? Mr. No time for a relationship? I would pay good money to see that." Devin laughs.

"Yeah, me too." I laugh.

CHAPTER THREE

"This one time in Vegas, my sister and I drank a few at the piano bar, then ran around the hotel playing doorbell ditch."

PEYTON

I'm browsing the calendar website and looking for next years' calendar. It's only the fall, and I've got plenty of time until I will actually use it, but I feel the need to buy something and this is something that makes me happy.

Hmmm, do I want funny, inspirations, cutesy with animals, half naked men or scenic?

I tap my chin and look at all my options.

I click on a few categories and scroll down the pages of the humor calendars, then I click on the landscapes.

Nothing is exciting me, which is odd, because calendar shopping is one of my favorite things to do. Every year, I have at least ten calendars in my cart and have to force myself to narrow it down to at least two. One for my office and one for home. Sometimes, when I'm feeling extra fun, I get myself a small desk calendar too full of quirky quotes.

I'm not instantly drawn to one calendar over the other. *This is frustrating.*

I open another tab, then go to my favorite planner company. Maybe a planner over a calendar will spark my joy. I'm strangely not in a calendar mood.

What am I looking for? Do I want vertical or horizontal days?

Why is this such a difficult task? This is not something that has ever been an issue. Why is it now?

I love to pre-plan my planners and calendars.

I decide to give up my search for the time being and stand up from my desk that's cluttered with paperwork, folders, and to-do lists. My normally organized office is far from it, maybe I need to get some more coffee.

As I walk past cubicles and co-workers, I notice that a few of them quiet when I get near or they stare openly at me, then quickly look away when our eyes meet.

It's weird.

Do I have a sign on my back?

Is there something on my forehead?

Omigod, am I wearing my skirt inside out?

I check off my rampant thoughts as I think them, and nothing seems amiss of normal.

Is it all in my head?

I pour myself a cup of coffee, the smokey cinnamon aroma steams off the lip of my cup as I inhale a satisfied breath with a smile before heading back to my desk. Walking the same path back to my office and feeling self-conscious, with my eyes set forward.

I pull out my mirror from my desk drawer and do a quick once over and again, nothing is out of place.

A knock at the entryway of my office pulls me from my thoughts.

"Hi, um, Peyton," Dana, my boss's assistant pauses. "Mr. Frederick would like to speak with you."

I stand smoothing out my skirt and follow behind her with a notepad in my hand as she leads the way, looking nervously over her shoulder, then offering me a forced smile.

Mr. Frederick motions to sit in front of his desk but doesn't speak to me right away. His fingers fly across his keyboard and then he clicks on his mouse before sitting back in his chair and looking me over.

"So, Peyton, how was your weekend?" he asks.

He's never asked about personal time away from work, so why, after three years of working here is he starting now?

"Um, well, sir, it was fun, I guess." I reply uneasily.

"You must know that I'm not one to dive into people's personal lives, but when it affects business, then I really have no choice, do you understand that?" he asks.

I slowly nod, unsure of the direction that this conversation is going.

"It's been brought to my attention that there are some interesting images of you on social media. Now, I would never fault someone for having a life outside of work and to each their own what is done on someone's free time. But, two of our largest clients have made some inappropriate comments about you and the type of employees that we have here. Since we cater to families here at Perfect Planning, I want to make sure our employees' image is not, well negative."

"I'm not entirely sure what you're saying, sir?" My mind tries to wrap around what he's telling me. I haven't posted any pictures, but I haven't been on social media since being back from Vegas.

"You went to Las Vegas last weekend, right?" He folds his hands in front of him on his oak desk awaiting my answer. I can tell in this moment that he's not mad, but more annoyed with having to have this conversation.

I slowly nod my head, unsure just what images he could be talking about. I haven't been on any social media since returning, so anything could be up there.

He turns one of his monitors, so I can see.

There is my Facebook page, with images that I appear to be tagged in. I'm dancing on top of a table, wearing a very short dress, holding a bottle of vodka. My face is slightly flushed, and I'm smiling. Quinn is in the background of the photo and so is the guy that I woke up next to talking to one of his friends. Hanna must have taken this picture.

Instantly, I'm embarrassed as I cradle my head in my hands.

I cannot believe this.

"Sir, my friend posted this." I say awkwardly feeling my skin blush from embarrassment.

"I can tell, since you're the prime subject of the image." He deadpans with a hint of comedy.

"I'll make sure that it's removed from my profile right away, I'm so sorry that this is interfering in any way." I say quickly to appease him.

"I'm not asking you to change your lifestyle. I'm also sorry that we had to have this conversation. But can I please ask that you make your profile private. I don't know why our clients were looking at your page, but then again, I also do not understand much of what people are doing or are into these days. But we do deal with children and families and I know that you speak with a lot of them at some point."

"Yes sir. I will do that right away. I'm sorry for any lack of distrust or comfortability this situation may have caused."

"You're not in any trouble, so please don't feel as such. But I just want to keep up the image of our company as a positive one, especially right now. We're all allowed to let loose, but let's just keep that in our private lives, shall we?"

"You got it. I'll change that right now." I say standing quickly. "Is there anything else, sir?"

"No, that will be all. Thank you, and again, I'm sorry about asking you to do this," he replies.

I head back to my office, grab my phone immediately, and open Facebook.

There I see it was in fact Hanna who tagged me in the photo.

I sit down and begin going through the motions of un-tagging myself and making sure that all my settings are private. I go through posts and change the audience, and once I feel that I've gone back far enough, I feel better about it all.

Three hours later, the photo is still there, but I've done what my boss asked of me. I've been productive, but not with anything having to do with work.

I've researched everything that I could find about Vegas weddings, and it turns out that what happens in Vegas after all, doesn't stay there.

But maybe I can just pretend.

MAXWELL

"You don't remember? How could you not remember? You and she were practically humping one another's legs in the VIP section." Conner tells me with a laugh.

"I faintly remember a woman, but I was two sheets to the wind man," I reply.

"No kidding. I don't think I've seen you let loose that much since college, I think you were even more wasted than Marcus."

"I agree. I was hungover as fuck, one would have thought it was my bachelor party" I say quietly.

"Well, you know some people do go to Vegas to get married, you sure you didn't do something like that with this hot chick?" Conner teases pointing his water bottle in my direction.

"I wouldn't do something as reckless as that. You know me, I think things through a little more than that." I shake my head.

"While that's true for sober Max, maybe blackout Max is a little more fun and daring."

"I'm fun. I'm daring." I cross my arms over my chest in protest.

"Sure, what did you do last night?" Conner asks.

"I worked late, came home and worked out."

"Last night, I found a speakeasy and played strip poker with Japanese twins."

"Not all of us live the kind of life you do. Some of us work for a living," I point out.

"I work," Conner says irritated.

"You're a social media influencer, you take selfies with products," I throw back.

"And I make money off of it, anyways, this isn't about me. Do you remember anything about her?"

"I keep getting flashbacks to the night, but nothing substantial."

"Anything good?" He wiggles his eyebrows.

"This conversation is over." I wave him off.

"Maybe you should get a private investigator if it's bothering you. I've got a guy."

"You have a guy for everything, but no. I'm good. I think."

"If you change your mind, I've got you."

We eat the rest of our meal in silence before Conner leaves and I'm feeling confused.

It's true. I don't let loose like I did while in Vegas.

I work a lot, but that's only because I'm not dating anyone.

I don't drink to get wasted, except while in Vegas.

————

SHE'S UP AGAINST THE DARK HALLWAY.

The walls are vibrating from the bass in the club.

She tastes like cherries and vodka with a hint of mint.

She moans into the kiss as her chest pushes against mine while my fingertips thread into her dark hair.

My hands move down her body and I dig my hands into her sides as we press our bodies against one another in the heat of passion as our bodies are energized in this moment.

The next moment, we're in a town car and she's straddling me. Her warm center is pressing against my slacks and my cock is aching to get nearer to her. She's as close to me as she can be, but I want more.

I need more.

I must have more.

I dart up in bed, sweat dripping down my face and my heart racing a mile a minute. I swing my legs over the side of the bed and take a deep breath with my palm sliding down my face.

Holy shit. That was one damn hot dream.

Who was she?

Is that her?

Is that the woman from Las Vegas?

————

THE REST OF THE WEEK, I'VE THOUGHT A LOT OF ABOUT WHAT Conner said and about my dream.

I should do a little more than work and I should get out and meet new people. And I have been remembering a little more about the woman that I spent time with in Vegas. She did sleep over, and I'm only assuming that means that we slept together. If the time we spent together was anything like my dream, I can only imagine what happened that night.

I still cannot picture her face too clearly, but from what I've been told is that she's beautiful.

I want to know more.

And I want to know what happened that night most of all.

I text Conner and ask him for his contact with my knee bouncing in anticipation. When I don't receive a reply after a few minutes, I shake my head and stand up. I walk over to the floor to ceiling window adorning one side of my office and look out at the view of downtown Seattle.

My cell phone dings on my desk and I fight to immediately dive towards the object. With my hands in my pocket, I walk over to my desk, lean over and look at the screen of my phone.

Conner's name shows up indicating there's a message from him.

I grab the phone and slide my finger across the screen to unlock it.

In the message is everything that I would need to know in order to contact the PI. I weigh my decision of whether or not to call the guy. But I don't waste any time and make the connection.

The guy had a last-minute cancellation and I luckily will have a meeting with him tonight, which makes me both excited and nervous.

What do I hope to gain from this?

What if I don't like what he finds out for me?

But what if I do?

CHAPTER FOUR

"This one time in Vegas, I ended up earning $100 on a stripper pole."

PEYTON

Speed dating is not something that I should be doing. But it just so happens that the holidays are coming up and this lady needs a date to the company holiday party.

However, as exciting as the mere thought of speed dating is, it's also horrifying. How can one decide whether or not to date someone that they speak to for five minutes?

I've spoken to five guys and I'm exhausted.

Dating is tough.

"Hey there, pretty lady. Come here often?" A twenty-something man jokes as he slides into the seat in front of me.

He's cute with dimples and a crooked smile. He leans forward and puts his head in his palm awaiting my answer.

"Hi, I'm Peyton." I point to my name tag.

He leans back in the chair and points to his. "John. So, Peyton what brings you to speed dating? You certainly don't look like you would need it." His eyes look me up and down.

I feel uncomfortable with the perusal. He does it in a creepy way that makes him look like a slime ball. But this is a part of the experience, right?

"I'm busy, I don't have time to date in the conventional sense."

"The conventional sense? What's that mean?"

"So, tell me a little bit about yourself?" I ask him.

"Well, what do you need to know?" He asks.

"For starters, let's talk about what you do?" I ask him.

"I am a club promoter," he says.

"What's that mean?"

"I promote events at the club that I work at. I coordinate guest lists, and make sure that the events get seen. What do you do?"

"I work for a party planning company," I smile.

"Oh, that's cool. So, we're kinda in the same field. Party and events are quite the same."

"Quite." I nod.

I think that our jobs are two different things. I know that I'm not going into detail about exactly what I do, but I don't hand out flyers.

The bell rings and it signals that the guys are supposed to move on.

"Well, John, it was a pleasure speaking with you."

"Indeed. I hope to see more of you."

The next guy and the next don't do anything for me, and while it was a fun experience, I don't plan on making plans with any of the guys that I met tonight. Whether it was bad breath, or just a complete lack of sensitivity of topics, I'm done for the night.

I walk in the front door to the sounds of loud moaning.

I press myself up against the closed front door and cover my eyes with my hand, even though there's a wall separating the front entry way and the living space.

"Quinn! If you are entertaining in the common area while naked, I have my eyes covered in case naked bodies need to run into the bedroom where these kinds of activities should be taking place!" I yell.

The moaning stops.

I listen for any movement, but I hear nothing for a few moments until I hear her laughing.

I pull my hand away from my eyes and see Quinn standing in front of me, fully clothed.

"What is happening here?" I ask. "You're fully clothed. Oh geez, are you soaking your fingers?"

"That sounds completely gross, like I'm marinating my fingers." Quinn laughs.

"Okay, how about dialing the rotary phone? Or strumming the lady parts' guitar strings?" I offer, still not moving from my spot against the door.

"I'm watching porn," she explains.

"Why are you watching that in the living room? Isn't that more of a private kind of show that you watch?"

"It's research, not for fun."

"Research?" I question stepping further into our apartment.

"I've been assigned to write up a story about the different forms of porn. Like the best of the best."

"You were assigned?"

"I bitched and complained during a meeting recently saying that all the fun and sensational topics were going to Gary, the suck-up. So, to my pleasure, I was assigned to this." She shrugs.

"And what are we learning?" I fight the laughter from erupting.

"That the women are clearly overacting, and the guys will do anything to stick it in all the holes. I've got some popcorn, care to watch some with me?"

"You're getting paid to watch porn." I shake my head while I drape my purse strap around the chair and walk over to the fridge.

"I am, isn't it great?"

I rummage through the fridge and pull out a few ingredients to make dinner.

"I think I'm going to pass on the communal porn watch party. I kind of am turned off by the male population at the moment."

"Aw, why is that?" Quinn says with a tilt of her head.

"Speed dating."

"Does your husband know?" Quinn jokes.

"Funny." I roll my eyes.

"Yeah, so something came in the mail today," Quinn walks over to the coffee table.

I glance at the television screen and see an orgy taking place and laugh.

Quinn hands me an envelope with an embossed city symbol on the envelope.

"State of Nevada, what the heck?" My eyes widen and I look up at her.

"You're asking me? Why would I know. I don't have X-ray vision."

I slide my finger to open the envelope and peek inside then my mouth drops open.

"Oh, oh, wow." I whisper before handing over the envelope to Quinn. She pulls out the thick paper and unfolds it.

"Your marriage license." She looks up at me and whispers.

"I do not remember any of this, how is any of this possible?"

MAXWELL

"Sir, I'm nearly done with my investigation and I truly want to thank you for this opportunity for a change in pace."

"Yeah, no problem. What did you find out?" I ask him impatiently.

"Well, it's rather quite a tale of your time in Las Vegas. I have to ask, you truly don't remember any of this happening?" He looks up from his folder and asks.

"I've gotten flashbacks or memories, but I'm not sure if they're real or not."

"This isn't nearly as entertaining as those Hangover movies, but let's see, where do I begin." He says to himself flipping through his folder of paperwork.

He pulls out images from security footage and spreads it out in front of me.

She's breathtaking. She's wearing a short dress with killer legs and her hair is long and straight. She has high cheekbones and a straight nose, with a slight upturn, but not one to make her look snobby. She has curves that are easy to grab onto, from the looks of my hands on her and it would appear that we are quite cozy.

She is dancing on a table with a bottle in her hand. I'm standing in front of her holding out my hand to her with a smile.

Another image is with the very same woman, sitting on my lap and my head snuggling into her neck.

The other has the two of us walking out of the club hand in hand.

"This is you and the woman—"

"Does she have a name?" I ask cutting him off.

"Ah, yes. I'm sorry. Her name is Peyton Manning, she's twenty-seven and lives in Los Angeles. And no relation to the football player.

"Peyton." I say her name quietly, liking the way that it rolls off my tongue.

"So, Peyton and you were seen leaving the club alone. After a few dozen phone calls around the city and getting into contact with the company of the town car services, you two went to a liquor store and purchased snacks, then asked to go to one of the cities chapels."

"Chapels? What?" My head snaps up.

"It would appear sir, that you and Peyton exchanged vows." He thumbs through his folder and places another series of images in front of me.

The photos are grainy, but I can clearly see myself and the woman beside me leaning toward me looks similar to the woman in the photos from the nightclub. Then more images that appear to be taken from someone at the chapel, such as one of the wedding packages boasting to be professional images with us glassy eyed and looking like we're posing for prom pictures.

We're clearly being married by Elvis, and we have a string of witnesses in the room with us, but none of them appear to be my buddies.

What the actual fuck!

The investigator then places a marriage certificate in front of me.

"The chapel had a service where they did the filing for you. Have you checked your mail? You should have received a certified copy."

"I have my mail held and delivered weekly. I haven't received it yet. So, this certificate is real and not fabricated?" I ask.

"Yes, sir," he nods.

"Shit."

"I take it that you do not know this woman, still?" He asks placing a clear image of her on top of all the others.

"I mean, she's vaguely familiar, but that could just be memory recognition. Is there anything else that I need to know about? Anything about her specifically?"

"She's clean. She has no record, she comes from questionable parents, but it appears that she didn't follow in their footsteps.

She has no criminal background and it would appear that you are her only husband, ever." he smirks.

"Thank you. Are these my copies?" I ask pointing to everything that's on the table.

"Yes sir. I included a profile to her as well, which will include contact information. Inside the folder are your whereabouts for the entire time-period that you were questioning. I spoke with employees and their statements are inside as well. I do have to say, again, that this has been a very entertaining case."

"Yeah. Well, at least for one of us it was. Thank you though, for being so detailed with your findings as well as quick." We both stand and shake hands.

"My pleasure. Mind if I ask, what are you going to do with all the information?"

"Marinate with it a bit before being hasty, that's for sure."

"Smart man. It was nice to do business with you. Should you have any additional needs, please let me know."

I'm left alone which is exactly what I need right now.

I'm married.

I got married in Vegas!

What do I do with this information?

CHAPTER FIVE

"This one time in Vegas, my friend and I went bar hopping with a guy we met working at one of the hotels. At every bar we went to, my friend told everyone that the guy and I were newlyweds and we drank for free all night. It was even funnier because she didn't drink !"

PEYTON

"I would like for you to accompany me to Seattle for the conference," Mr. Frederick said upon my entering his office.

He didn't let me sit, didn't ask how I was doing, or even a hello.

I'm frozen in place in the middle of his office, clutching onto the notepad and pen that I carried in here.

"Why?" I ask. I clear my throat and correct myself. "I'm sorry sir, I didn't mean to sound so spoiled right there. May I ask, why you are requesting that I go over your assistant?"

"Because she is unable to attend, she has personal obligations to tend to. Plus, I feel that it would be good to finally start adding new offices. We've got an amazing brand, we're well known here in California and why not tackle the Pacific Northwest?"

"You want to open up other offices?" I ask.

"It's been an idea that I've been tinkering with, yes. You are the glue of this office, and I value your input."

"Sir, I'm the office manager. I order pens and keep everyone happy." I point out.

"Is there anything that would create an issue with you joining me on this trip? It will be Wednesday and Thursday, traveling back Friday morning and you can have Friday off?" He says ignoring my protest.

"Trying to sweeten the deal?" I smirk.

"Maybe," he smiles.

"Fine, I'll cancel my kickboxing class."

"Perfect. I'll have Dana send over travel information before the end of the day. Now, I have one more favor to ask?" He pauses and stands up.

"Sir, if this is about my social media, I promise you that I did as requested."

"Not at all. But thank you for doing that. We're going to need to rearrange the schedule of the Foster Family Reunion. I received a message that they are planning to change everything, including dates due to something with one of their business's and timelines. Last minute things, can you get on the horn and make sure we have the staffing and whatnot?" He asks.

"Of course, sir. I was meaning to get in touch with graphics to make sure that we had their new logo, for branding."

"Good, thank you. Do you need anything from me? How can I help make your job easier?" he asks.

I give him a devilish smile.

"Well, I would love to speak to you during our trip about an all staff event, you know the party planners, throwing a work party?"

His face lights up at the idea. "You know, it's been a while since we've done something like that, good idea. Make a list, and we'll discuss it during our travels."

At home later that night, I'm packing for the trip when Quinn plops herself on my bed.

"Since when do you go on work trips? I think the most that you've traveled was up to San Francisco."

"Since my boss's assistant couldn't go and I'm the lucky runner up," I deadpan.

"You'd always be my first choice," Quinn flips onto her back and says in a light tone.

"Yeah, yeah, yeah." I shove socks into my bag.

"So, where are you going?"

"You will never believe it," I stop moving around and look over to her.

"Somewhere fancy?" She quirks her eyebrow.

"Seattle."

"Shut the front door!" Quinn's mouth drops open. "Are you freaking kidding? Seattle? You and your husband will be in the same place at the same time. Are you going to go find him? What are you going to say? Oh my God, can I come?"

"Slow your roll, crazy bitch. I'm going to Seattle for work. Not on a scavenger hunt." I laugh.

"Are you kidding? It would be more like a treasure hunt. I mean think about it, he would be a damn nice prize." She barely contains her laughter while I roll my eyes.

"I'm not going to stalk the guy," I say.

"He's your husband, you have every right to."

"He's my husband, I don't even know him."

"Girl, he wrecked your lady bits. I think you know him."

"You are infuriating," I shake my head and continue packing.

Our Uber driver dropped us off under the beautiful arch of the Washington Convention center at 7th and Pike. I look across the street and see a grill across the way and on the other side, a Cheesecake Factory. This area looks nice and the convention center is popping with foot traffic. We walk through the doors and turn to the left to walk up the stairs, following the banners alerting us to where the convention is being held. We head up the elevators to the Sky Bridge on the fourth level, I look up at the arch overhead and gasp in the beautiful sight before me.

"This is amazing," I gush to Mr. Frederick. He offers me a smile as we walk into the exhibit hall which is even more beautiful with the tapered block ceiling.

The day is full of walking to and from booths, mingling with other professionals in the industry. I break away from my boss and attend a catering symposium while he attends a workshop on stationary. We leave the conference towards the end of the day and I'm exhausted. All I want to do is to go back to the hotel and soak my entire body in the jacuzzi bathtub. But Mr. Frederick wanted to go to dinner across the street instead.

Thankfully after dinner, I'm back in the hotel room in record time and lounging in the large tub.

My head is leaning back on the lip of the tub, my eyes are closed, and the jets are making me feel wonderful. I'm not sure how long I sat in the swirling warmth, but by the time I'm done— I don't even bother getting dressed and crawl into bed.

The next day is a day full of viewing properties in the downtown area and surrounding cities. At every turn, whenever I would see an attractive and well-dressed man in a suit, I would think about *him*.

What is he doing right now?
Where is he?

Does he know?

I won't deny that I looked up his office building and I also won't deny that I strategically scheduled viewings for locations around his building during the morning and lunchtime hours.

And I won't say that every second of the time that we were in the vicinity of his building that I wasn't looking over my shoulder just in case.

MAXWELL

I'm sitting in a window seat around the corner from the office with Cooper when I glance up and could swear that I see the woman in the photo from the Private Investigator. I watch as she and a much older gentleman walk toward the diner talking to one another and then pointing around the area. While holding property folders that I recognize from one of the realtors that I work with.

I shake my head. My eyes are playing tricks on me.

I've been staring at her photo and file so much that I'm seeing her here in Seattle when she lives in Southern California which is over a thousand miles away.

"What's up with you man, you seem kind of distracted," Cooper asks.

"Oh nothing much, just a lot going on." I shake my head.

"Bullshit, it's the middle of the month and you are always a lot more relaxed in the middle of the month. Spill it, tell papa what's on your mind?" He swivels his chair and faces me.

"I don't want to talk about it," I shake my head.

"C'mon, tell papa."

"Quit calling yourself 'Papa', it's kind of creepy," I push his shoulder.

"I'm not going to stop, tell me."

"Why are you begging like you're a gossiping teenager?" I look him over.

"I'm bored. I need to focus on something other than me,

because I'm just way too fabulous and need some heartbreak. You have heartbreak written all over you."

"Gee, thanks. I'm not talking to you, get over it." I turn back and gaze out onto the street.

The woman that I thought was *her*, is now no longer in sight and I put the thought of it being *her* out of my mind.

"Talk to, Papa." Cooper echoes.

"Motherfucker! Okay, so I'm married and all I can think about is her, I see her everywhere and she's in my constant thoughts." I say just as quickly as my thoughts run.

"No way, you got married? Congrats man!" He pats me on the back and then he has a confused look on his face. "Wait, when? Why wasn't I there? What's happening? I didn't even know you were dating anyone? Who is she? When can I meet her?" He spits out.

"Whoa, calm down there Janet!" I tease him.

"Who is Janet, is her name Janet?"

"You're impossible."

"So, wait, you're married? How did this happen?"

"Vegas." I say before taking a sip of my smoothie.

"When did you go to Vegas?"

"Seriously? You were there man."

"Um, I think that I would have remembered you getting married."

"Funny thing about that, you were there. Not the wedding apparently, but this happened during Marcus's bachelor weekend."

"That hot chick?" Cooper asks.

"You remember her?" I turn to him.

"Yeah, she was quite the looker. Young, tight, and you looked like you really liked her. You guys were totally all over one another."

"Well, so that night, I kind of blacked out and well, I got married."

"What do you mean?"

"It means that I fucked up and got married to a perfect stranger."

"And are you sure that it was a real marriage?" he asks.

"Why wouldn't it be?"

"What happens in Vegas, stays in Vegas."

"How have you managed to live this long?" I shake my head.

"Good looks, a large cock, and killer stamina." He says matter-of-factly.

"You're a complete dick, I hate you."

"So, how's this working, where is she right now? All lost in your sheets and passed out?"

"Well, she lives in Los Angeles." I tell him.

"That sounds like a shitastic marriage, when do you see her?"

"Funny story and I'm surprised that you aren't putting two and two together."

He shakes his head in confusion. "Not following."

"I got married, I don't remember it happening." I say with finality.

"What?" he looks puzzled.

"Sometimes, I wonder why we're friends."

"It's because I'm good looking, have a large cock, and great stamina," he responds.

"None of those things would be something that would impress me," I tell him, "this whole conversation is making my head spin. I should get back to the office."

"But you haven't touched your lunch,"

"I am willing to take it to go."

I stand up and carry my bowl over to the counter, leaving Cooper confused, but he stands up anyways and follows.

"So, does this mean that we can throw you a bachelor party?" He leans in and asks.

"No, man. I've got to figure out my next steps. But thank you for the offer." I lie.

I get my protein bowl packaged to go, head out of the diner, and walk towards my office building. I'm torn with what I should do.

I've been married for a month and only just found out. I'm confused and not sure what I should be doing. I am, however sure that I need to approach the fact that I'm married delicately.

What the hell do I do?

CHAPTER SIX

" This one time in Vegas, a unicorn was my maid of honor. "

PEYTON

My two days in Seattle were nerve-racking.

Everywhere I turned while in the city, I thought that *he* was around. I thought that I saw him in a window at some corner diner and I thought that he was standing in front of his office building.

It was almost like looking him up before the trip was a jinx and that was all I could think about.

The trip was a success and it looks like there may be a future of an office in Seattle.

Which is ironic.

After being in Seattle and paying attention to the lifestyle that people there live, it's faster than I'm used to.

Yes, I live in the City of Angels, but I'm not immersed in the flashy portion of it. I live in Echo Park and that's far from Hollywood, especially if you count sitting in traffic.

But, with being in downtown Seattle, I can feel the push and pull of the city, and by internet stalking *him*, I can tell he wouldn't live a slow lifestyle. Or at least, I wouldn't expect him to. His profiles show him in dress shirts and suits. His company profile makes him look like a badass and the fact that he's a partner, means that he's got little time for sitting around in sweats, eating his feelings and binging on the latest thing on Netflix.

What if we met, and he learned how I wouldn't fit into his life. How I'm too regular and not fascinating enough for a powerful businessman.

I will admit that I'm judging a book by its cover. But just by the looks, he and I are night and day.

I'm a freaking office manager for a party planning company, albeit a well-known one, but I'm an office manager. I live comfortably, sharing an apartment with my best friend. We regularly will eat a box of mac-and-cheese over a seven-course meal, hell a three-course meal, and we save up all of our money for Vegas vacations like the one we returned from recently for months.

The types of guys that I date don't wear three-piece suits, they wear jeans with flip-flops.

I spoon some ice cream into my mouth then sigh heavily. A light knock on my door interrupts my thoughts of despair.

"Hey, Hanna and I are thinking of going dancing tonight, do you want to come with?" She asks.

I look up at her from my pint of goodness, then look at my clothing.

"That would mean that I need to shower and get ready." I state.

"How hard could that be?" She puts her hand on her hip.

"Well, that would mean that I would need to get up from my

comfortable spot here on my bed. That I would need to shower, then get myself looking club ready. What would I wear?"

"Are you making excuses for not wanting to go out? You don't have to if you don't want to," she leaves it open ended to leave the decision up to me.

I put my ice cream down and sit up to cross my legs.

"I don't think I want to go, I'm feeling a little off after my trip and think that I'm going to just have a low-key weekend." I tell her.

Quinn steps into the room and takes a seat at the foot of my bed with a concerned expression.

"What's up?" she questions.

"Nothing, just a little self-doubt creeping in, nothing big. It must be that time of the month."

"Wanna talk about it?" she offers.

"Nah, I'll be fine. Just going to relax and do some self-care." I tell her.

Quinn smiles and then stands. "If you want me to stay in and binge watch something, I will gladly do that with you."

"Nah, I'm all good. But thank you."

At the end of my night, I'm sitting in the darkness of my room with my laptop while I watch Netflix on one side of the screen and have his picture that I downloaded from his Facebook page on the other side.

A girl can dream, right?

MAXWELL

When I was given her file, I may have stared at her photo a dozen times. I looked through all of her social media, and I didn't see anything that raised red flags anywhere even though the PI told me the same thing.

In fact, I scrolled through her Facebook page and nothing looked out of character. She posted funny memes, thought provoking articles and photos of her friends and herself. She was tagged in a few images that looked like they were from Las Vegas, but there was no indication that she would remember what happened that weekend from cryptic updates or what is known as 'vaugebooking'.

After sitting on all the information for a week, I decided that it was time to set some out of town appointments to check in with clients and to take a road trip down south. I'm not sure how long this impromptu trip will be, and I'm going in with no plan what-so-ever.

She lives in a suburb of Los Angeles, on a residential street that had both trendy looking apartments and small homes. When I pull up to her apartment complex, I sit parked on the street looking up at the building. It isn't much, it is a small complex, not completely updated, but at least it looks to be in a good neighborhood. There is a lot of activity in the neighborhood. There are people riding their bikes, there are small families walking toward the park at the end of the street and people outside their homes watering their yards.

I'm not exactly sure how long I sit in the car, but eventually when my thoughts began to get impatient with thinking of what I will say, I say '*fuck it*' mentally and get out of my car.

I've memorized the address and her apartment number, as I walk straight to her door.

I stand there, unsure of what exactly I'm going to say. I'm unsure whether or not, she will remember me. And a part of me, a part that I'm not used to, is uncertain of what will happen after I meet her.

I raise my fist to knock on the door and straighten myself as I pull my hand back without connecting it to the surface of her door.

Why I'm so nervous. I've faced tougher situations in the conference rooms with the management team. I faced harder situations face to face with my father when we didn't agree. I can talk my way into every conversation, but right now, I'm not sure that I can.

I breathe in and then release it.

But before I lose my nerve, I knock loudly on the door.

I hear someone shout something on the other end of the door and a second later, I hear the locks, then the door opens a crack. An attractive woman looks out through the crack, then opens the door all the way.

Her eyes widen and her jaw drops. No sound is coming out of her mouth, but I can tell that she is trying to say something.

"You're, you're… him?" She points at me.

"You know who I am?" I ask her shocked.

"You're him." She says in a gasp.

"Care to elaborate?"

"The guy from Vegas. You're the mystery man." she says loudly.

"Are you okay? Are you having a stroke?" I ask her.

"Mystery man is standing right in front of me, at the door and he's gorgeous I can't believe this. Pey, is going to flip her lid."

"Standing right here, hello." I wave.

"Well, shoot. You should come inside. You look exhausted."

"Thanks. So, Peyton knows about me?" I ask.

"Only what we've read about you on the internet. She doesn't remember Vegas and well, kinda is avoiding the fact that you guys are married."

"So she knows?"

"Knows what?" her friend asks.

"About getting married in Vegas." I'm losing my patience.

"Oh that, yes. She doesn't remember anything and you know what happens in Vegas stays there and all." She waves her hand to dismiss the whole thing. "Wait, you know about Peyton?" she stops.

"Is… um… Peyton here?" I ask following her inside the small apartment looking around at the space.

It's a mixture of chaos and organization. There's a large couch facing a bookshelf with a small television. The kitchen is a galley kitchen with multi-colored cabinets and a small circular dining table off to the side.

The woman who opened the door and let me in is running around the small space picking up random things and shoving them all into a closet just inside the hallway that likely leads to the bedrooms.

"You're looking for Peyton? Aww, that's so cute." She shuts the door and approaches me clasping her hands together in front of her.

"Well, yeah. And you are?" I ask her.

"Oh, I'm horrible. My name is Quinn. Pey and I are roommates."

"So, Peyton?"

"Oh, she's went to the store right quick."

"How long do you think she will be?"

"She's, um, been gone for a bit, so I wouldn't think too much longer?" the woman says looking anxious.

"Do you mind if I stick around?" I ask.

"Not at all. Have a seat," she points over to the small table and moves toward it.

"Thank you. So, did we meet previously?" I ask, feeling embarrassed that I have to ask the question.

"Yes and no. You were pretty zeroed in on Peyton. I did more talking with one of your other friends, but you and I didn't have much interaction. So, you must have been pretty loaded too? You don't remember getting married?" She asks talking a mile a minute.

"Wait, were you there?" I ask.

She shakes her head. "No, Hanna and I went to get drinks and use the ladies' room, and then when we came back, you two were gone. We tried to get ahold of her, but she turned her phone off, or something."

I run my hand over my face. At least neither of our friends were witnesses to this whole thing.

"Are you here to whisk her off and away, like Prince Charming?"

I scoff at the idea.

I don't whisk women away.

"To be truthful," *What am I doing here?* "I'm here to get down to the bottom of whatever this is. I'm not sure what happened that night in Las Vegas, but I'm pretty sure that I didn't intend to come home married to a stranger."

"She doesn't remember either, remember?" She pulls out a chair and leans toward me with her chin in her palm, a doe-eyed gaze and smiles.

"What?" I ask.

"You're so much better looking that the internet shows."

"I'm glad you think so," I say awkwardly.

I hear the key in the lock and I stand suddenly, even though there's a wall that is blocking my vision of her. I can feel my heart beating out of my chest and I think that I've stopped breathing until I hear a bunch of random songs mashed together in the worst singing tone that I've ever heard.

CHAPTER SEVEN

"This one time in Vegas, I tapped a famous baseball player on the shoulder while I may have had a lot of alcohol in my system then proceeded to push him out the way so I can go to the bathroom."

PEYTON

"Oh, we're off to see the—anaconda don't want none unless—you let me see that thong, th-thong, thong, thooooooong!" I don't hold anything back, my voice cracks as I let the last of the Thong Song go extra-long. I pride myself in making my own mash-ups, and this one, is one of my best. I've kicked shut the door and bring the bags from the store into the small kitchen and place them on the small counter space that we have.

"Oh shit, I'm sorry. I didn't know you had company, please excuse my horrible—" the guy looks familiar and suddenly it's as if someone threw a ball straight to my gut, "it's you." I whisper.

He smiles, and it's the kind of smile that makes you want to tear off your panties and throw them at him.

"You must be my wife?" He says stepping forward, looking the epitome of calm, when I'm anything but. He holds out his hand and smiles.

I place my shaky hand in his and give a slight wave with the other.

"Hello, Wife," he grins.

"Hello, Husband," I return quietly.

"How long have you known that we were married?" He asks cocking his head to the side.

"Truthfully?" I pause.

"I wouldn't have it any other way."

"Since I woke up in your bed, naked and rushed back to my hotel room."

"You didn't think to wake me up and share the news with me?"

"You could have been a serial killer. I watch the ID channel. I know that I need to stay sexy and not get murdered."

"I think that if you spent the entire night with me and were as naked as I was when you woke up, you wouldn't have survived the night. I too, watch the ID channel and know that you need to stay out of the woods just the same."

Quinn sighs. "Look at you two, that's already a few things in common."

I look over to her and give her the evil eye.

"Listen, I'm sorry. I woke up and remembered nothing. I didn't know that I was married and thought you were just part of a dream. Can we start over?" He asks shoving his hands in his front pockets, looking suddenly, very boyish.

"Right. Sorry. I just wasn't expecting to see you, or rather meet you and then here you are."

"Well, a proper introduction should be done then. Hi, I'm

Maxwell Addison, and you are?" He holds his hand out to me once again.

"I'm Peyton Manning, and no I'm not a football player or have any relation to his family. Also, I do not play any sports." I smile shaking his hand again.

The corners of his lips turn up and I think I've just fallen in love with my husband.

"I THINK YOU NEED TO GIVE HIM A PROPER CHANCE," QUINN whispers.

I'm standing in my closet while Maxwell sits in our living room. I've agreed to go out to an early dinner with him and truth be told, I'm terrified that I really may start to like him and then my heart will be broken because we live so far from one another.

I can't do a long-distance relationship, and that's all that it would ever be since we live in different states.

But I'm getting ahead of myself. I must control my thoughts and I must just look at hanging out with the guy as a means to get out of this sham of a marriage.

"No proper chance, Quinn. He's totally not my type. And even more importantly, I live here and he lives somewhere else. He's fancy suits and I'm worn in sneakers."

"True, but he came down here for you."

"Yeah, to get me to sign divorce papers, not whisk me away. This isn't a fairytale."

"Maybe he should take care of you, you know with orgasms, and lots of them. You sure that you can't remember any of that night together?"

"I'm pretty sure that if I did, you would be the first one that I would tell."

"That's a good point."

I pull out a cute black dress that's not too slutty looking and not too fancy at the same time. I wore it for a work party once and I recall getting a lot of compliments from it.

I slip into the dress, do a quick brush up on hiding any bags from under my eyes, throw some lip gloss on and put my hair up in a purposeful, yet messy twist.

I turn around for Quinn and smile.

"How do I look?" I ask her.

"Ready to impress your husband for a night out on the town," she replies confidently.

I walk back into the living room where Maxwell stands looking through our stacks of books that grace almost the entire wall.

He looks over at me and I can see his eyes dilate as he turns to face me.

"You look," he looks like he's trying to find the appropriate word, "divine."

"You make sure that you have her home, at some point. I'm just kidding, our girl here is a full-grown ass adult and has no curfew." Quinn jokes handing me the small handbag that I pulled from the closet and pushing me toward the front door.

"So, what do you do for a living?" he asks after we've had our order taken.

"I work for a party planning company, I don't do anything fancy, but I run the office here in town." I reply, trying to make my job so much more than what it is, knowing how high he is at his company.

"What kind of parties do you guys throw? Corporate or birthdays?"

"We do it all. We have both a familial department as well as a corporate one. We cater to all. We're actually trying to expand offices up and down the west coast. I think one of the locations will be up in your neck of the woods."

"As in Seattle?"

"The one and the same." I nod.

"And how exactly would you know where my neck of the woods is?" His eyebrow shoots up with a side smile.

"Ugh, because, I would just assume that you're, uh, up north. You have a Seattley-vibe to you. Okay, okay, we stalked you a little."

He ignores my admitting to the internet stalking and asks, "what kind of vibe is that?"

"You know. The kind that likes to drink coffee, throw some fish around and then wear flannels." I say nervously.

"I hired a private investigator to help me figure out that night."

"And, what did he tell you, because it's all still a little hazy to me."

He runs through the details of the night. Starting out at the club, where it's assumed that we met, to when we ditched friends to getting married by Elvis. After that, there's sparse details aside from us entering his hotel together holding hands and making out in an elevator, which leaves the rest of the night until the morning blank, but likely very eventful.

I blush at that last bit and avoid eye contact with him.

"So, about this whole marriage thing, what do we do about all this?" I ask reaching into the purse on my lap, pulling out the ring I woke up with and pushing it toward him.

MAXWELL

She's gorgeous.

She's awkwardly gorgeous and I'm not completely sure I want to let go of her just yet. I'm not sure what my intentions were when I saw her. But I do know that I want to hold onto whatever this fairytale is before completely giving it up.

"I'll be here in town for a week, how about we get to know one another?" I offer her.

What the ever living fuck?

I'm staying a week?

Where did that come from?

She looks taken aback by my offer, which is rightfully so as she presses her hand to her sternum. Her lips form a tiny little "o" and I'm imagining improper things that I would like to do to this stranger.

Technically, in the biblical sense, she wouldn't be a stranger. I woke up naked, and I'm pretty sure that if I asked her, she did too. So, I'm thinking that we did some things that would make us more acquainted than we seem to recall.

While it's been a few months since the trip to Vegas, my body is amplified around her, so while I may not recall much, maybe my body's reaction to her is telling me something. Something that I should pay attention to.

"You're here for a week?" She asks.

"I am. I have clients here in LA and I purposely scheduled appointments, so while I'm out of the office—it would appear that I'm not fucking around. I can still bill for the time away from my actual desk and make any surface a work station." I explain.

"Are you always so detailed and serious about work?" she asks.

"I have to be. I deal with clients that are high in stature. I need to present myself as the utmost of professionals and that means making myself available."

"What if your clients caught you at an opportune moment?"

"I wouldn't put myself in that situation. There are times when it's clear that I'm conducting business. Other times, such as during the Vegas weekend, I left my cell phone in the hotel room. Probably a dumbass idea for that night, but I did wake up with two phone calls on my phone that looking back, I'm glad I didn't answer."

"I see. So, Mr. Maxwell Addison—" She begins, but I cut her off.

"Please, call me Max. Maxwell is so formal, and I would prefer that we get to know one another on a different level after all this is not a business transaction. I'm not buying your company and you're not planning one of our events."

"Ok, so Max, tell me about yourself? You say we should get to know one another, so let's do this?"

"I wasn't saying we have to know everything right now." I tell her.

"Foundations. Let's learn about foundations. Tell me, how did you grow up?"

"Wow, hitting hard. That's easy. Parents wanted more for me than they had themselves, but they wanted my sister and I to work for it. I got scholarships for college and started at the very bottom of the company during my junior year of college. I worked my way up thinking that it would impress my father, but I never knew whether or not it did. But I must have been doing something right. Once he passed, his recommendation was to name me partner, so here I am." I say as quickly as possible.

"And your mother?" She questions.

"My mom is still around. The crazy old bat still tells people that she's thirty-five and she's happily living in Florida at one of those old folks communities."

"Are you guys close?" she asks.

"I see her a few times a year, my sister and I take turns visiting her, so she's not too lonely and talk to her once a week, but that's about it. What about you? Tell me about your upbringing?" I ask.

"Once upon a time, there was this girl. She had a mom who

liked to drink and a dad who liked to gamble. One ended up dead, the other is in jail. That's about the gist of my story," she says, as cryptic as possible.

"So, who raised you?" I ask.

"I did. I'm an only child, so were both my parents. So, I don't have much in the ways of family. I wasn't really an orphan, my mom died when I was sixteen and my dad got beaten up a lot, left me on my own many nights. But, it wasn't until I was actually eighteen, and still in high school, that the cops caught up with him. After he went to jail, that was that and I didn't keep in touch. He got out and never looked me up, like I didn't exist. Don't worry, when we get a divorce, none of my family will come out of the woodworks looking for anything from you." She has a sad look in her eyes when she relays the whole story, as short as it is, it's whole and I doubt there's much more that one would care to know. But when she mentions divorce, it makes me sick to my stomach. I don't think that's what I want.

Dinner is delicious and the company, was a lot more than I was expecting. I didn't think that coming down here to Los Angeles would amount to anything other than preparing to get a divorce, but now, I'm not entirely sure that is what I want to do.

She's a lot more than what she would seem. She's humble and hard working. She doesn't ask for anything and doesn't strike me as the kind of person that would take advantage of another.

So, I told her that I would be here for a week and I was sincere in saying that I wanted to get to know her.

Except, I think I want to get to know her in a more than friendly way.

She intrigues me.

She turns me on.

And she definitely isn't a bad choice as a life partner, from what I've seen in the few hours that we've been reacquainted with one another.

CHAPTER EIGHT

"This one time in Vegas, I spent all day drinking and never got drunk."

PEYTON

Maxwell is charming. But I know from reading romance novels and watching rom-coms, most assholes and pricks are. So, there has to be something underlying there that would turn that button on for him.

He is way high up on the totem pole of his company and here I am, likely making a quarter of what he makes. He's champagne and fancy appetizers that are slimy, and I'm a pigs in a blanket with Doritos type of gal. We are complete opposites.

But opposites sometimes attract.

And he's definitely attractive.

Like I would lick his cheek and likely cream my panties in result type of attractive.

Spending the evening with him was reminiscent of a first date. We shared tidbits of our lives, our pasts, and laughed about the small things. While dinner with him, made him a little more human to me and not just something super unattainable, it's still very clear that we are from different worlds.

We parted ways last night with him giving me a kiss on the cheek and making plans for lunch today. He was coming to pick me up from work and that's all I knew.

So, I sit nervously in my office googling topics to talk about during a lunch date and coming up empty.

I've dated plenty in my life, but this whole thing feels so different.

He wants to get to know me. *Why?*

He hasn't brought up the word divorce. *Why?*

He's here for a week and intends to see me every day that he's here. *Why?*

I wasn't aware that I wasn't alone until a folder is placed on top of my keyboard.

I look up and see Mr. Frederick staring at me with a concerned look on his face.

"Hi, um, sir. What can I do for you?" I say standing up, my movement pushing my office chair back to slam against the wall.

"Are you okay? You getting enough sleep? You looked almost as if you fell asleep, when I first walked in here." he asks.

I shake my head, "no sir, I'm sorry. I was just brainstorming new concepts for a corporate event that we received a bid for this morning. Anyways, what's this?" I pick up the folder.

"It might be for the corporate party that you were daydreaming about." He grins.

I open the folder and nod.

"I started working on a profile for them already, I spoke with one of the owners this morning. The owners are new and wanting a relaunching party." I tell him.

"Who do you have assigned to this project?" he asks.

"I haven't assigned anyone yet, I was going to look at the details, but I haven't gotten to that yet."

"Good. I'm assigning you to this."

Shock flows through me, I'm not the party planner point person, I'm behind the scenes. I run the orders, make sure things are where they need to be, same with the people. I order office supplies, for crying out loud. I do not throw the parties or events.

"I'm sorry sir, what?"

"I want you to take the lead, I want to have you more immersed in the business, in all facets." He tells me confidently.

"I'm not understanding," I shake my head.

"Just trust me on this. I see something with you, and I have plans for your future. You're the lead, run with it. Schedule those in person meetings, make sure you tour the spaces if they have one. You know the drill, you made up the check list. Ask me any questions that you may have. But I want you in on this."

Still standing, I'm a bundle of nerves, but I smile anyways— despite the fact that I want to jump out of my skin.

"Sir, I will not let you down." I hold out my hand and we shake.

"I JUST AM SHOCKED, I DON'T KNOW WHAT HIS PLANS ARE, BUT it's like suddenly, I have a new position in the company and I'm not sure what to do with it." I take a large gulp of the beer in front of me.

"Is it something that you want?" Maxwell asks me.

We're sitting in a booth, both of us with full beers, waiting for our lunch orders.

"I don't know. I don't think this was something that I ever thought about. I'm not an in front of the party person, I'm someone who likes to do the other stuff, the behind the scenes crap." I am on the verge of hyperventilating when Maxwell stands and comes to sit beside me in the booth. My breaths are moving in and out of my lungs quickly. My eyes are wide and holy shit, what is he doing? His presence right now is not helping.

He wraps his arm around my shoulders and pulls me into him.

He smells delicious, like a fresh shower and eucalyptus. I lean my head against him and breathe him in as I calm down.

It must be the eucalyptus.

Koalas get high off of the stuff when they nosh on it, I must be getting high from the smell.

I doubt that it's the close contact and his strong arms.

I'm not sure how long we sit here, enjoying one another's embrace.

"Thank you. I'm good now." I say leaning back to look up at him.

He licks his lips and looks down at me. The nearness of him is making me dizzy and I'm definitely not expecting what happens next.

MAXWELL

My knuckles graze her cheekbone and my body has taken over control, shutting off my brain and all rational thought.

I lick my lips, lean down and our lips touch. Gently at first as my hand wraps around her neck and up into her hair.

The start of the kiss is getting used to one another. I've caught her by surprise with the kiss and she doesn't fully let go into the kiss until I lightly bite her lower lip. Her hand is on my thigh and I'm silently begging for her to move it up.

Our tongues tangle and our heads tilt in opposite directions as we explore one another's mouths, until plates are placed on the table loudly by our waiter.

We pull away from one another, her eyes immediately dart

away from my gaze as she pushes away from me letting a foot of distance between us on the booth.

She tucks a strand of hair behind her ear and clears her throat.

"I'm not sorry about that," I say preluding what she's likely thinking. She looks at me, her lips parted, but says nothing.

"I'm sorry that I took advantage of your panic, but I'm not sorry that I kissed you." I tell her.

"Okay," she says quietly.

"I told you that I wanted to get to know you, and that includes in whichever way," I say.

"I think that our situation is a little more complicated though," she says.

"We can't annul the wedding, we would have to get a full divorce, why rush it?" I ask.

"You can't be serious?" her hand with a French fry freezes mid-air.

"If we get a divorce tomorrow or a month from now, it's the same thing." I shrug.

"A month from now? You realize that we live in two separate places."

"Is this our first fight? Over when to get a divorce?" I grin.

"I mean why fight the inevitable?" She asks. "We can't stay married."

"Yes, yes we can."

"No, Maxwell, we can't."

"Please, no more of this Maxwell stuff. Max, please? It sounds so formal. Considering that our tongues were just in each other's mouths, you don't need to be so formal."

"You're impossible. Listen, you're acting hasty, I think this low elevation has gotten to your brain," she tells me.

"I don't make hasty decisions—well, Vegas was one thing—but I don't make hasty decisions. I think it would be nice to get to know one another. Something drew us together that night—"

"Yeah, alcohol." she interrupts.

"Besides that. Maybe being married to one another can benefit us. I know that, I have enjoyed your company and I like what I've gotten to know of you so far, what can it hurt?"

"How are you serious?"

"Listen, Peyton. I'm attracted to you. I'm not going to deny it, and if you're attracted to me—which that kiss kind of answered that—then let's take advantage of our situation. What fun is it to get a divorce when we're not entirely sure that is a good idea."

She must be a witch. I'm under her spell and I'm not sure what I'm saying anymore.

She looks to be contemplating my words.

"Okay, let me get this straight, you want to date me?"

"I think that would be a good way to put it," I nod.

"And what about the fact that I live here in Los Angeles and you do not?"

"Easy. There's this form of transportation that was invented that makes traveling long distances easy. I can come to you and you can come to me. During the work week, there's video calls or whatever. I'm here for another six days, and like I said, I want to see you, a lot while I'm here."

"There's no long run here, I work here and you work there. I sincerely doubt that as a partner you can just up and move to Los Angeles. And I think it would be presumptuous that I would drop my work and friends here to move to where you are."

"Let's not make those type of statements this early on in our marriage. We take this one day at a time. Hell, there's the small possibility that you may not like me overall."

"What about you not liking me?" She asks.

"Not possible. I already do." I reply confidently before taking a bite out of my burger.

CHAPTER NINE

"This one time in Vegas, my friend and I spent two hours getting ready and my friend stepped out of the elevator into a pool of vomit and fell down into it."

PEYTON

He wants to date me.

He wants to stay married and date me.

Having that conversation at lunch was a little surprising and left my head spinning.

I do my best with trying to concentrate while at work, but for the life of me, I'm pretty much Googling him and trying to find as much information on him that I can.

I switch over to Facebook and there's a friend request on there.

From him.

Why is he friending me?

I accept his friend request and note that what Quinn and I were looking at was most definitely the public version. His feed is littered with personal stuff. He has friends, some of which look vaguely familiar posting articles and tagging him in photos. Some of which are from Las Vegas, but nothing looking too debaucherous.

There was a group image though, and there I am, sitting beside him. His arm is wrapped around my waist and my hand is sitting comfortably on his thigh. We're leaning in together, smiling. Both of our set of friends are in the photo, and there's a few bottles of vodka on the table in front of us.

The image was posted less than twenty-four hours ago by someone named Jason with a comment saying that this was found on his cloud.

I see the last thing that was updated on his profile is that he changed the relationship status to 'married' from single. There is a whole slew of comments of congrats and confusion underneath.

This change was made an hour ago and I'm not sure how I feel about it.

Shaking my head, I click through his photos, and notice that he does have a laid back side.

Today, he was wearing a dress shirt and dark jeans and while he wasn't dressed in a suit—he still looked like he was working.

It's interesting to see this other side to him. He's commented on a few things here or there but hasn't had a status update in a few weeks aside from his relationship change.

———

"So, you're going to start dating your husband?" Quinn asks while I prep dinner for tonight.

"Apparently so. He said that there's no difference in getting a divorce now, versus getting a divorce a month from now." I say chopping up vegetables.

"So, you guys are going to stay married? How will that work with you guys living in two different places?"

"I don't know. We're winging it." I shrug.

"And tonight, you're making him dinner?"

"Yes, so, if you can maybe hang out at Hanna's for a few hours?"

"Oh girl, I'll do you better. I'll pack an overnight bag." Quinn stands to her full height, turns on her heel and basically skips towards her room.

I finish prepping the meal for tonight and just as Quinn is leaving, Max walks in. He surprises me walking into the kitchen with a bouquet of colorful wildflowers. He comes to my side, and gently kisses my cheek.

"Do you have a vase?" he asks.

I have my hands covered in enchilada sauce and point with my elbow to the cabinet behind me.

"Top shelf."

He follows where I'm somewhat pointing to and manages to select the correct cabinet on the first try. I hear the water run and then he's unwrapping the flowers. He runs the stems under the spout and uses a knife to cut them at an angle before placing in the vase silently.

Once he's finished, he places the vase in the center of the small table and then turns to me.

"Hi," he says leaning against the fridge.

"Hi," I reply dousing a tortilla and then grabbing some of the mixture.

"This looks like a lot, you know we could have ordered food, right?" He pushes off the fridge and looks into the bowl.

He's very close to me and I feel an uptick in my heart rate immediately.

"You can't come to Los Angeles and not have some authentic Mexican food."

"Is this a family recipe? I wasn't aware that you are Hispanic?"

"There's a lot about me that you don't know. But I'm only part, my father donated the Hispanic genes to me. My mother was from here. But this is a recipe that I got from the internet, I've never made it before, so let's hope it comes out good."

"How do you know that I'm not a vegetarian?" he asks.

"Because of the two meals that we've already shared together, you've eaten meat during both. So, I believe that it's safe to assume that you will eat this meal."

"Paying attention. That's good. So, how was the rest of your day?" He comes to stand on the other side of the counter, so we're facing one another.

I finish getting dinner ready and we make small talk in between. Once the buzzer goes off on the stove, Maxwell springs up first and heads towards the kitchen. He fits his hands into the oven gloves and reaches into the oven to pull out the casserole dish.

He sprinkles the last of the cheese that I had sitting out and replaces it in the oven then returns to the couch beside me. With a grin, he turns to me.

"See, I can cook. Reason number ten million to give whatever this is a chance," he says.

"I'll need to start writing this stuff down."

"Now, let's talk about something serious. Who is your favorite sports team?"

MAXWELL

Since I've been here in Los Angeles, I've definitely not acted like myself.

I've been aloof, insecure and spontaneous.

Back at home, I'm serious, busy, and have no time to have

lunch outside of the office. I have no desire to date and I definitely do not practically beg a woman to give me a chance.

But here I am.

Fixated on the woman that I drunkenly married during a blackout. Asking her to hold out on wanting to get divorced and saying that a long-distance relationship can and will work, despite my past and the unknown.

What our future holds?

Fuck! Who knows.

The last time that I dated a woman, we were both workhorses as I just got named partner and we would occasionally get together to eat a lunch or fuck. I'm not completely sure if that can be called a relationship, but the past few years have been busy.

But here I am, sitting on this woman's couch, after eating the most delicious meal that I've had in years and wanting nothing to do but get to know her better.

Who the fuck am I?

My hand is on her knee and we're sitting close.

She's resting her head on her hand and has a happy smile on her face.

"So, tell me what brought you to Vegas that weekend?" I ask her.

"My friends and I have wanted to do a girls weekend trip for a little bit. We just never had our schedules line up. But then once it did, we jumped at the chance. What about you?"

"My buddy's bachelor party, you know, the typical excuse for a bunch of guys to go there. Most of us went to college together, so in a way it was like a reunion, even though half of them, I still see on a regular basis."

"Do you drink as much as we did that night?"

"Not at all. I will have a drink usually after getting home from work, but there's no blackout drinking like that night." I reply shaking my head.

"And you don't remember anything from the night?" She leans in.

"I've had glimpses here and there, but not vivid details. I had glimpses of you and possibly what we did, but your actual face was never really that clear. At least, until I had seen a photo of you."

"And you got one from a private investigator, one you hired because you lost 24 hours of your life?" She grins.

"It was haunting me. I'm glad that I did, receiving a copy of our marriage certificate out of context would have been shocking."

"You got one too?" she stands up and rushes down the hallway, then returns with an envelope.

"Yeah. We requested that the chapel file it." I tell her matter of factly, just as my PI told me.

I look it over and smile.

"So, a marriage in Vegas is true and binding? I mean, we're married, for real?" She asks as if she still can't believe any of this has happened.

I nod and try to change the subject, so I can lengthen my time with her.

"So, Mrs. Addison, I can go back to my hotel, or we can watch a movie?"

"I haven't changed my last name," she tells me, "what kind of movies do you watch?"

"I'm cool if you want to keep your last name, I'm not a total dick and I really don't have a preference. I watch documentaries and some random true crime shows on Netflix."

"We got married while wasted, I think the married thing is still fresh and yes, if I did get married, I would hyphenate or keep my last name for sure. I can get down with a thriller, that's a little true crimey." She replies and I'm enjoying the two topics we're covering.

"Darling, whether you believe it or not, we're married. It's legit." I hold up the marriage certificate and then get an idea, "I've got a better idea. Let's go for a drive, are you up for that?" I ask.

She looks at me for a long moment then nods.

Moments later, I'm starting the car with a general idea of where I want to go, but I still ask her to type in Venice Beach into the navigation. Once we're on the road, I casually rest my hand on her knee and she does nothing to push it away, she even leans toward me, with her knees pointed in my direction and her elbow resting on the center console as she looks out into the early evening.

Once I navigate through traffic and find parking, I offer her my hand and we walk together toward the beach, past the tourist shops on the boardwalk, past the outdoor gym and before we get to the sand, I direct her to a bench and we pull off our shoes. I roll up my jeans and offer her my hand again. She takes it without hesitation, and we walk across the sand stopping at the water's edge.

I drop my shoes beside my feet and take a deep breath.

"Care to sit?" I ask her.

"You're going to get sand everywhere." She drops her sandals and drops to the sand.

I follow suit and sit as close to her as I can.

I drape my arm over her shoulder and pull her into me naturally. She doesn't pull away, even leans into me.

This moment, the smell of the salt in the air, the sounds of waves crashing and seagulls flying overhead, and the texture of the sand between my toes. I want to remember this moment forever, as we relax into one another's embrace.

"I want you to come to Seattle. I've seen you in your element, I would like for you to see me in mine." I say to her, looking out over the water.

"Are you as carefree as you have seemed to be here? I wouldn't have pictured you in jeans or wanting to sit on the beach. Based upon your job and all."

"I can occasionally be casual, but work is mostly suits and not as lax. I will admit my place overlooks the bay, and while it's a great place, I don't take part in visiting much of what Seattle has to offer. Part of me feels us getting married that weekend was part of the plan for me, somehow. To let loose and to ease up on the working myself to death. I love what I do, but I also have noticed that I don't take the time to enjoy my time when I'm not at work."

"Since you work a lot, does that mean that you don't make time for relationships?" she asks pulling apart but still sitting beside me looking out to the horizon.

"Not as much time as I should. I think that I'm understanding now that I have been greatly lacking in a few areas of my life. I have you to thank for that." I say playfully, bumping my shoulder into hers.

"Why me?"

"Because, if it wasn't for you, I wouldn't have known that there was a deficiency in any of my life."

"Oh wow, that's a good line." She smiles gazing ahead at the water as it breaks on the shore.

"I just thought of it myself, so, my question, you never answered, will you come to Seattle, maybe next weekend?"

"About that, I don't know if you are aware, but I likely make a significantly less amount of money than you do, and I don't just have expendable money to take last-minute trips. I plan out trips well in advance, like months in advance."

"I realize that, and I'm prepared for it. Like you said, I make money, and considering the fact that I do not want to wait months to see you again after my week here is up, I will happily fund your trips to Seattle."

"Sounds like a business transaction and so one way. Tell me, what is your plan here? We fly to one another every other week-end? You pay for everything, all the gallivanting—that just seems unfair."

"Let's play it weekend by weekend. I have to start driving back home on Sunday, to be back in the office Tuesday morning. How about this, a true test to any relationship is a road trip, any chance that you can take Friday and Monday off of work?"

CHAPTER TEN

"This one time I partied with the Mayor watched him fall off a stage drunk, get back to like a pro and then partied the rest of the night with Kool And The Gang!"

PEYTON

His question shocks me.

Hell, everything that he's said to me since meeting him has shocked me.

He wants to date or get to know me. He doesn't want to immediately put an end to whatever this is. This accidental marriage.

And now, he wants me to be in Seattle.

I'm not entirely sure if I could take the time off so soon, but every part of me wants to say yes.

"I just got this new event that I need to start, I don't know if taking a four day weekend would be the smartest option right now." I finally say.

"What if I told you that I can help you out with that?" He asks with a mischievous smile.

"I'm not following," I look over to him.

"What if I told you that I know the company who likely hired yours, or at least I have an idea of a few companies who may have hired you?"

"What?" My mouth drops open and my head swings his way.

"I suggested your company to a few of my clients as I was meeting with them this week. You know what I do, right?"

"You buy and sell companies." I reply robotically.

"In about 90% of the companies that I work with, they are looking to throw events after their final steps of the takeover, it's a rebranding or relaunching of the new company. Since now, I know someone specifically in that business, and especially here in LA, I can refer these events to your company."

"Are you the reason why I was named as the planner for the one that I was assigned?" I ask, feeling my anger boiling.

I don't need any handouts and I definitely do not need him interfering with my job.

"Not at all. I introduced myself to the owner, your boss as a heads up that I was hoping to send business his way, said that I was a friend of yours and you mentioned that your company does corporate events. I swear, that's all. I told him that I would like to partner with him by letting my clients in the area, know about what you guys offer. And that's all I did. I only said your name with the introduction. I didn't say anything else." He holds his hands up.

"But you talked to my boss." I push away from him and stand up. I begin to pace on the sand in front of him. He stands up and halts my movements by placing his hands on my arms. He bends slightly to look me in the eyes.

"I did. I felt that it was professionally important to give him a heads up. I should have called him before I mentioned your company, but luckily, he was thrilled with the references. I swear to you, I did it with all honest intentions. I didn't think that doing so was doing something forbidden."

"And you told Mr. Frederick that you know me?"

"I said that we're friends, I didn't think that it was my place to tell your boss that you got married, I don't know the relationship there."

"When did you talk to him? Was it as soon as you came down here? When your PI reported back to you?" I need to know if expanding our company is because of him.

"The other day," he replies immediately.

"And you've never talked to him before this?"

"Not at all. Why?" He looks confused.

"We went to Seattle a few weeks ago for a conference. While we were there, we looked at office property. I didn't know how the two would connect." I shake my head, not fully understanding what my train of thought was.

"Wait, you were in Seattle?" His hands drop, and he stands up straight as I nod. "And you were aware that we—about me?"

"Yes."

"And you didn't think to maybe find me? I know that you've looked me up, you knew the address of my building."

"I did. But what was I supposed to say, 'hey, I'm your wife and it's nice to meet you?'"

He smiles but doesn't say anything.

"What?" I ask him.

"You just said that you're my wife," he shoves his hands in his pockets.

"Well, yeah. Remember, we have the marriage certificate." I roll my eyes.

"All night, you've been adamant on avoiding the fact that we're married, and you just now said it."

"Ugh, Max. Can we just go? The beach sucks right now." I say crossing my arms over my chest. I feel frustrated and I'm sure I'm over reacting, but I just need a moment and getting away from the beautiful beach, where we shared a pretty great hug, I just don't want to tarnish this memory right now.

"No. We're not done. Why didn't you come and find me?"

"I was scared. I thought that because we had gone as long as we had between Vegas and when you showed up, that you couldn't care less. That you wouldn't be interested, and that well, the fairytale of being married to someone like you would have been over just as quickly as it started." I look down as I bury my toes in the sand. "You were the hot guy in a tux, I wouldn't have ever spoken to you if my friends didn't dare me. You are out of my league. I guess, you would have thought that I was some crazy chick."

He steps in front of me and pulls my hand into his.

"Never. I mean the jury is still out on the craziness, I think we need to continue to get to know one another. But never, would I have turned you away. It doesn't matter whether or not your status in life is the same as mine to be with me. I want to determine that factor. I want us to determine that together. You're beautiful. Any man would be a fool to turn you away. So, yes, Peyton, if you haven't gotten it yet, I'm interested. And I would have loved it if you came to my door and told me that you were my wife."

He takes my breath away as he bends, and his mouth covers mine with one hand cradling my jaw and the other wrapping around my waist pulling me against him. My arms dangle at my side before my body fully reacts. I move my arms around his neck and melt into him.

Into his kiss.

. . .

MAXWELL

"Bornnnnnn to be wiiiiiiiiillllllllld!" Peyton sings off-key as I cruise up the freeway.

She head-bangs and plays the air guitar as she moves her hips in her seat. After the beach the other night, and once I calmed down and gained some perspective, we relaxed into a comfortability with one another.

She's not shy of the fact that she can be a goofball, she knows that she sings horribly, but does it anyways, and even though her friend Quinn warned me about Peyton's lack of remembrance of charging her phone—I did receive a text from her roommate saying her phone was dead and to have Peyton to call her. I am fascinated by her and liking every little bit of what I'm learning about her.

We're almost to Seattle, just passing the state line into Washington and she's kept me entertained the entire trip. She's begged to drive throughout our drive, but a gentleman always drives his lady around. Each time I've told her that, she would protest by sticking out her lower lip and crossing her arms over her chest, pushing up her tits in her tank top and making my mouth water.

I don't know how my last minute thought of her coming home with me was made possible, but I'm not going to question anything.

Her boss gave her a few extra days off and set her up with a few more viewings of properties while in Seattle for their possible office expansion. The thought of her company opening up where I am excites me, but I down play my feelings of it as we're still a fresh relationship. Plus, I don't want to jump to conclusions about it being her who comes to Seattle to run the space.

"Oh my God! I think I can see the space needle!" she yelps.

"We're still several hours out, I think you are seeing things." I smirk.

"Then what's that?" She asks pointing to something in the distance." I follow to where she points and laugh.

"That's a cell phone tower."

She slinks into her seat and mumbles an *'oh'*.

My hand rests on her thigh as we continue to drive. She starts to sing again, she tells me made up stories, and she even exhausts herself and nods off. I pull into the garage of my tower and slip into my parking space. I cut the engine and turn to her.

I lightly shake her shoulder, "hey sleepy-head, we're here." I say.

She slowly wakes, blinks rapidly and sits up.

"Where are we?" she asks.

"I've taken you to an undisclosed location, where I plan to chop you up into pieces," I grin, "we are in the parking garage of my building."

"What time is it?" she unbuckles her seatbelt.

I open my door and slide out of the front seat just as she does the same.

"It's almost dinnertime, speaking of which; we'll need to order something. What are you in the mood for?" I open the trunk and pull out our bags.

"I could eat a horse, so whatever you want is fine with me."

"Liver and onions, it is!"

"You wouldn't dare," she places her hands on her hips playfully.

"I'm not going to lie to you, but I eat out a lot. Half the time, I'm not even home. So, I'm well versed in takeout."

I wheel her bag with my duffel resting on my shoulder and I point in the direction of the elevator banks. We ride the elevator to my floor and enter into the foyer of my home. She walks into my space, past the wall separating the living room from the dining room, and straight ahead to look at the view. The clicking of nails across the kitchen floor alerts her attention to a furry creature approaching her.

"And who is this?" she asks bending down to greet Scout.

"My best friend, Scout." I say proudly.

She pets him for a few minutes and then stands again to look at the view.

Peyton stares at the sunset over Elliot Bay as the lights to the Big Wheel glitter across the water. She walks quickly to the floor to ceiling window and presses her hands against the glass. She pushes away and quickly turns to me with her hand over her mouth and eyes wide.

"I'm so sorry, I didn't mean to touch the glass," she says.

I prowl toward her, wordlessly. I leave my expression neutral and back her up. I bracket her body between my hands as I press my palms against the glass.

I lower my head and I brush my nose against the delicate skin of her neck. She inhales as I reach her ear and gently bite her ear lobe. After a light tug, I release her and my hand grazes the side of her body.

"You can dirty up my windows all you want." I whisper against her lips.

I press my lips against hers, with my tongue grazing across hers as she returns the kiss. Her hands wrap around my neck as she pulls me into her. With our bodies pressed against one another, we continue to make-out against the glass of my home. Until I pull back, her cheeks are flushed, and her eyes dilated with passion. She's breathless and wordlessly grabs my hand and walks over to my couch. She pushes me to a sitting position and sits astride me as my hands immediately fall to her hips.

I lean my head back against the couch and look up at her. With my right hand, I brush her hair away from her face.

"You are breathtaking, absolutely breathtaking, Mrs. Addison." I whisper, smiling up at her.

She cups my face with her hands and leans down to kiss me. It's a soft kiss at first, hesitant, as we're still new and she's unsure of how much dominance she can unleash.

Our tongues lash against one another and I melt into the cushions as all of my senses are filled with her. Her touch. Her taste. Her presence alone is making my thoughts move from purely passive to aggressive. I want to tear off our clothes and I want to lay her down on the couch. Instead, I pull my head back slightly, breaking the kiss.

"Food," I whisper against her lips. "We haven't eaten since Portland."

"You mentioned takeout? What's good around here?" She asks quietly, her lips returning to mine to lightly brush against them, sending jolts of want and desire through my body.

I have to get up, but I don't want to. Having her so close to me is all I want right now, but I need to remember that she's not going anywhere, at least not if I can help it.

As if reading my mind, she smiles and presses her fingers against my mouth. "To be continued," she promises, "but feed me otherwise, you're not going to like me anymore."

I laugh. *As if that is possible.*

"What happens?" I grin.

"I turn into a moody teenager, and teenager Peyton, you want nothing to do with. She's a total brat and very stubborn." She leans down for one gentler kiss then moves to sit beside me.

"Food, okay. Sustenance, I can do this. I just need one minute here before I get up." I say, willing my cock to soften and not make me look like the teenage counterpart.

She looks down at my lap knowingly.

"It's okay you know, it might help my ego." She wiggles her eyebrows.

I laugh and shake my head, stand up, then adjust myself with her laughing.

"Follow me," I hitch my head over towards the kitchen.

I open my takeout menu drawer to a gasp from her.

"What the hell, this is the first of its kind that I've seen of this," she says.

"What?" I ask her puzzled.

"You have an entire drawer of menus, who does that?"

"Um, I do. I work a lot and don't cook. So, when I am home, I order in."

"Am I going to be eating alone while I'm here?" she asks nervously.

"I'm going to do my best to not let that happen, I promise" I tell her with absolute confidence.

And hope that I can keep my word.

CHAPTER ELEVEN

"This one time in Vegas, we drank for free at the same bar three nights in a row, because we were the best pole dancers on their public poles - but then we lost our friend then I threw up in their trash can!"

PEYTON

Seattle is amazing.

One moment it's raining and the next its clear skies, smelling fresh and looking as if Mother Nature scrubbed the scenery clean. Sure, it rains in Los Angeles, but not nearly enough. And besides, the landscape here is vastly different than there.

At home, it's a concrete jungle. Freeway upon freeway, with any true nature being in the canyons or an hour away with traffic. In Seattle, there's seasons and from the large windows of Max's penthouse condo, I can see city, water and across the bay it looks like a whole lot of nature.

We sat and ate kebabs from a Mediterranean restaurant on the couch with *Friends* on in the background. We didn't talk much, as the food was so delicious that I wanted to stuff my face more than anything. But it was a comfortable silence.

When we were finished with dinner, Max took out the trash and offered me his hand to pull me up.

"I still have to give you a tour of my place," he tells me.

"Right, I don't want to get lost in here." I grin.

His place is massive, too massive for just him.

"Well, you already know this area, the kitchen and the living room. That window has now become my favorite window," he points to the one that he pressed me against when we first got inside.

Hand in hand, we walk down a hallway on one side is a bathroom, and the laundry room. Nothing fancy, just standard living spaces.

On the other side of the hallway is a bedroom.

"Master bedroom," he says leading me inside.

There isn't much in the room. Just a bed big enough for a family and a nightstand. There's a picture over the bed adding a splash of color in the way of paint smatterings with the walls a muted white.

The bedding is charcoal gray with light gray pillow.

He's silent as I observe his space. I turn around and there's another bathroom. Obliviously there would be a master bath.

"We just started this tour, and I've already counted two bathrooms, what's the deal here. Did the people who built this place figure that there needed to be a bathroom at every turn just in case you eat something bad?"

He laughs and shakes his head.

"There's three more bathrooms," he says grabbing my hand and leading me out of his room and down the hallway. "There's a bathroom for every room, the one up by my room is the half-bath

—which is you know—for the whole place, and so people don't have to go into a bedroom."

"Where are we to the space needle?" I ask.

"The other penthouse on this floor has the view from one of its bedrooms. I've got the bay, while the other has the city. I think I got the better end of the deal." He grins.

Max shows me the other rooms, with one turned into an office and the other a small gym. As we walk back down the hallway to the main living area, he stops at the bedroom beside his.

"I'm not going to be presumptuous and force you to sleep in my room with me, so this can be your room. Since it's the only one that is furnished as a bedroom." I look to him, slightly disappointed, but also grateful.

We relaxed for the rest of the night. We were both exhausted from the long drive, but we didn't want to part just yet. So, we lounged together on the couch while we talked for a few hours before we eventually fell asleep in one another's arms.

"IT SMELLS HERE," I SCRUNCH MY NOSE UP AT MAX.

We're on our way to Powell's Seafood Restaurant for lunch before Max has to return to work.

"We're walking through the market area, of course it smells. What did you expect, it to smell like roses?" he says with a smile.

"Oh shuddup. How do they keep the smell of fish contained in just this area? Do they put air fresheners outside of the Pike Place area?" I ask seriously.

He stops walking as I continue a few steps. I notice that he isn't beside me and turn to look at him.

He looks amused. I walk back to him, tilt my head to look at him and smile.

"What?" I ask.

"Some of the things that you say," he shakes his head, wraps his arm around my shoulders and begins walking again. "C'mon, I'm hungry for some calamari."

Lunch was nice, and afterwards I walked back to his building with him. I recall standing in front of the building debating on whether or not to sneak a peek at him when I was here in town with my boss.

"What time do you think you will be home?" I ask him turning to face him.

He pushes a stray hair behind my ear and smiles. "I'll be home before dinnertime."

"We sound so domestic right now," I say with a laugh.

"Well, Mrs. Addison, I don't know about you, but I sort of like it." He leans down and kisses the tip of my nose, then moves his head and lightly kisses me. We're holding hands and I press into him briefly, still aware of where we are—I pull back before we get carried away again.

"I'll see you tonight," he whispers, his forehead leaning against mine.

"Tonight." I reply.

He squeezes my hand and we pull apart.

"Don't get lost in the city, don't talk to strangers, and don't go marrying another random stranger!" he teases.

MAXWELL

I don't know what is happening to me.

Since officially meeting Peyton, I haven't been the serious, business-driven hardass that I normally am.

I don't let up while at work, but I am a little more understanding of my assistant not completing a task than I normally would have been.

And for once, I pay attention to the time and look forward to going home.

Because I have someone to go home to.

I've never had someone waiting for me when I get home from work. I've never had someone that I worry about if I would be late. And I've never made it out of the office before six in the evening.

It's five-forty-five when I walk into my condo, and it feels different than when I normally come home.

My home actually feels like a home, with the lights on and a delicious smell wafting in the air. This type of thing, hasn't happened for years—I'd almost forgotten what it was like. I place my laptop bag and keys on the island and see Peyton standing in front of the stove stirring absently in the pot, with her other hand petting the top of Scout's head as he sits loyally by her side, hoping for her to drop some food. The dog pays me no attention, which means she must have used her witchcraft on him too. I walk up behind her and kiss her on the neck. She cranes her head away as I lay another kiss just below her ear.

Scout's tail wags as I also reach down and pat his head. There's so many new developments happening right now, that I feel like I'm in an alternate universe—something that I could get used to.

"What's cookin' good lookin'?" I ask.

"I'm making Bolognese. How was your day?" she asks.

"It went by pretty quick, but it was good. I liked having the lunch break away from the office, that's something that I could get used to."

"Yeah? Where do you usually eat lunch?"

"If I'm not schmoozing new clients, which is still considered work and we talk more than we eat, I'm eating at my desk."

"You know that isn't healthy, you should take time away from your desk."

"Yes, mom."

"Ew, don't call me that." She playfully swats me.

"Yeah, that's pretty gross, the things that I want to do to you, are disgusting things to do with your mother."

"The things you want to do to me?" She quirks an eyebrow.

"You have no idea." I growl.

We haven't taken the relationship that far yet, and I'm letting Peyton be the one to guide how fast or how slow we go. We've done a lot of kissing, and a little bit of grinding, but all of our clothes have stayed on so far.

I feel like I'm back in high school.

I've given her the option to sleep in the other room, and so far, this hasn't been something we have had to face with passing out on the couch last night.

"Dinner will be ready in about thirty minutes, do what you normally do when you get home from work." Peyton turns back to the stove. "Which would be…"

I observe her again with a smile. Scout is back by her side, waiting for something to drop on the floor and she's oblivious to my perusal of her.

"I usually work out, shower and then continue working." I reply.

She looks back at me. "You come home from work, to only work more?"

"I like to get ahead of things. I'll be back, I'm going to shower the work day off of me," I wink at her. Her face flushes and she turns back to the stove.

"Thirty minutes, Buster." She warns.

"Yes, Ma'am."

Not much longer after I disappeared, I'm returning back to the delicious smell of dinner. Peyton has plated our food and is filling wine glasses that I wasn't aware that I had with red wine. I slide into a chair across from her at the table and place my napkin on my lap.

She looks expectantly at me confusing me as to what's happening.

"Is everything okay?" I ask.

"I'm waiting for you to try it," she explains. "Sorry, I don't mean to be creepy about it. This is my favorite recipe and I always like to capture the first bite on new people."

I nod, feeling a little self-conscious, but give in and get some of the meal on my fork, bring it to my mouth and have it attack all of my senses in the most amazing way. I linger with the taste and chew slowly as my eyes roll into the back of my head. I'm not exaggerating but experiencing this moment. I'm not sure how much time has gone by, but by the time that I've come back to planet Earth from what was like heaven—Peyton is digging into her own plate.

"Did I have all of this in the fridge?" I ask.

"Not at all. I've never seen an empty fridge. I mean I have, like when you first move into a new place, but it looks like you've never used the thing. And that's a really nice fridge, how could you not use it. I'd kill for a fridge like that, although back home, I'm pretty sure I would get robbed if someone saw it in my kitchen. No, it would be the entire kitchen, that thing is huge." She rambles.

"I take it that, you're finding your way around the city?"

"There some cute stores around here, expensive as hell. But totally cute. I also asked the downstairs guy and he pointed me in all the right directions."

"You didn't need to go and spend your money," I tell her.

"How else would we eat? I'm only here for another three days and I'm not going to eat takeout the whole time. While it's good takeout, I can cook some things, and your kitchen is made for cooking."

"Give me a list of things that you will need and I'll have the food delivered." I tell her.

"I think I got enough to last, maybe even make you some things for when I go back home."

That thought saddens me, but I shake it off and try to change the subject.

"So, I have some good news," I begin, "I work all day tomorrow, and can't get away for lunch, but the following day, I have off and we can do whatever you wish."

Her smile takes over her face and she's almost bouncing in her seat at my news.

"Anything?" she asks.

"Anything," I tell her.

CHAPTER TWELVE

"This one time in Vegas, each time we walked the Strip, the strip club and escort girls would give me their pamphlets and brochures—ignoring everyone else in our group, including our single guy friends."

PEYTON

I have everything that I want to do written as a list on my phone. I mapped out everywhere that I wanted to go, and kept it a secret from Max. It's been hard to do so, though.

Last night, he came home and after we ate dinner, he tried to tickle torture me until we ended up wrapped up in one another like crazed teenagers.

We've slept in separate rooms, despite the want and desire building up, but I've wanted to get to know him before I planned to sleep with him—again.

We get into the elevator and before he can press for the

garage, I press for the street level and he looks at me with a confused look.

"I have my plans and it doesn't entail that we drive around in your car." I tell him holding up my phone.

"So, how will we get to wherever that you want to go?" he questions.

"Public transportation and our own two feet." I smile. "They're made for walking you know."

He nods slowly and then looks at his feet.

"And that's just what they'll do. Good thing that I'm wearing my comfortable shoes." He rolls back and forth on his feet. "So, where to first?"

I open up my phone, smile and point up the street, away from the bay.

"We are fifteen minutes away from our destination," I turn my face to him and smile.

"Walking, right?" He asks.

"Yes, we can take an Uber or something after that, but I would like to walk around the city a little bit. You can see so many different things from the walking perspective that you can't in a car."

"Wherever you go, I will follow." He grabs my hand and we start on our journey.

We take in the smells, the good and bad of Seattle. When Max almost stepped in dog poop, I nearly died of laughter with the disgusted look on his face, and then laughed even more when he actually did step in dog poop not five feet later. After cleaning off his sneakers in a nearby public restroom, and with Max likely silently cursing me for making us walk at first.

Not much longer, I came to a halt on 4th Avenue and stare up to the sky at the building in front of us.

"What's this?" Max asks.

"Columbia Center. They have a sky view observatory and it's

supposed to have killer views. Since being in your place, I'm all about these views." I grin.

Once we're high up, with a panoramic view of Seattle, my breath is taken away. We have a view of everything from the mountains to the bay. It's breathtaking and beautiful.

"Let's take advantage of where we are, care to get a drink and something to eat?" Max asks trapping me in his arms from behind. I lean back and smile.

There's a bar behind us, with an eager bartender waiting for us to come up to him and order something.

"I could go for a little something," I reply.

We each get a beer and share a BBQ Chicken flatbread then admire the views.

Before leaving, Max pulls me to him and lowers his head.

He kisses me softly and pulls away.

"I want to make sure that I kiss you at every place we go to today," he says quietly.

"Um, okay. Any particular reason?" I ask searching his eyes.

"Because I want everywhere we go, to remind me of you when you go back home. So I can look back at a location like the Columbia Center and remember that I kissed you here."

"Ooooh, you're good. You're too, too good, Mr. Addison," I push him playfully away.

"On the contrary, Mrs. Addison. You're the first wife that I've ever had, I only save my cheesy lines for you." He grins pulling me by the hand back to the elevator.

While it's fun that he calls me 'Mrs. Addison' at any chance that he has, I do wonder how serious he is about that.

"So, you have offhandedly mentioned that you work a lot and you don't have time to date. But do you date?" I ask.

"I haven't had anything serious, that I can recall. Aside from you. Does that scare you?"

"Well, I don't know to be honest. I don't know what the future holds for us. We live in two different states, we are two vastly different types of people, and we don't know that if this fun thing we currently have going is anything lasting." I say with as much confidence that I can manage.

The elevator silently slides down and we've made it to the bottom floor in moments.

"This way," I point as we walk hand in hand in the direction that my plans have sought for us, he doesn't ask where we're going, but he does reply to what I said in the elevator.

"Any relationship has its questions and obstacles. It takes two to make it work. One person can't be doing all the heavy lifting. Sure, you're a little more easy-going and care-free than I am, but that doesn't mean that one can't even the other out. I think of it as a perfect balance, in other words a completion."

"Don't go quoting Jerry Maguire on me!" I point my finger at him and warn.

"I like you. I went down to LA, not knowing what I was going to come face to face with when I saw you. But I like you. It could be the fact that we're opposites, and I am totally okay with that. Yes, we live in different cities, but there are ways to bypass that. The amazing things that are done with technology these days. But for fun, would you ever move away from Los Angeles?" he asks in all seri-ousness.

"I've never thought of it. My job is there, my friends are there, my entire life is there. I don't know anything different. It's never been a topic of conversation that I've ever had to deal with while in a relationship."

"And what if it came down to that a year down the road. We're tired of the back and forth, we wouldn't be able to have a successful marriage if we're living in two different places," he points out.

I nod my head slowly. "I see that as being something that

would be a pretty big obstacle. Would you consider moving to Los Angeles, possibly opening up an office there?"

"Like you, this is new territory for me. I've never given Los Angeles much thought as a place to live, but I'm not going to say that it would be out of the question. If we completely fell in love, and that's what you wanted, me to move to LA, then I would."

He takes my breath away with that, as that's exactly the thought that's been in my head too, during this entire conversation.

I stop in the middle of the sidewalk and turn to him. I reach up and pull him down as I meet him on my tippy-toes. His arms wrap around my middle and he bends then lifts me. My feet dangle as he kisses me, leaving me breathless when we pull apart.

"I'm going to assume that I said something right, to warrant that," he asks.

"It's like you're in my head, you basically said out loud some of the rampant thoughts that have been circulating in my head."

"So, what you're saying is that we're a little bit alike, after all?" He grins.

"Maybe just a little." I say as he sets me down.

He looks around and questions, "where are we going?"

"Are you ready for some history?" I ask.

"It wasn't my best subject in school, I was more of a math guy."

"We're going to learn the history of Pioneer Square, but not from the surface. From below."

"I'm sorry, what?"

"It's basically underground tunnels that we're used in the late 1800's and during the gold rush days. It's like a whole crap ton of history that we will be given a tour with."

"And it's here, in Seattle." He asks.

"Yup." I nod excitedly.

"How do you know these things?"

"I've done my homework." I reply.

Once we check in, and join the group for the tour, we're off underground and then above ground within two hours. We would have been out sooner, but Max had a million questions that kept the very insightful tour guide on his feet.

At a few places while underground, Max would linger back from the group and take a moment to kiss me sweetly, with a quiet note of 'for remembering'.

Once we emerge on Main Street, the fresh air awakens me as the bright sky blinds me. We thank our tour guide and say our goodbyes and begin on our way.

After an Uber trip, we're dropped off at the Space Needle. I've only seen it on television, it's bigger than I was expecting, but defiantly not as big as our first stop of the day. I look to a dome-like glass structure and I have a sudden change of plans.

"What do you say about, instead of going to the Space Needle, that we go there instead?" I ask him pointing to the structure.

"I think that's a garden, I'm up for it."

We walk in and look up at the creations of color. The explosion of color and beautiful art created throughout the space is breathtaking and something that I'm so happy that we came here for instead of going to the Space Needle. We take our time walking through the small space and looking at all the towering displays of glass.

Over an hour, we've spent here, immersing ourselves in the experience that once we leave, we both feel like new people.

I look at him, and he looks just as happy as I do.

MAXWELL

I see a lot of places, a lot of attractions in the city day after day, but nothing quite like the things that Peyton planned for us today.

I've lived here in Seattle for my whole life and not once did I ever stop to see some of these places before, outside the car and on my own time. It's like I'm enjoying the city for the first time, and I can't believe that I've missed seeing my home this way.

With Peyton being here, I've been a tourist today in my own city. She's made it easy and effortless to explore. Despite stepping in dog crap, it's been an excellent day. Peyton has made it so easy to do everyday normal things and so far, she's brought out a different side of me. A side that not that many people can bring out.

The human side.

When normally, I would rather get a ride back to my condo, I suggested that we walk back to my place.

Hand in hand, through the streets back to The Emerald. We make small talk, with her talking more than I and I couldn't be in a better headspace. Until she asks about my past relationships. I know she is concerned about the long-distance thing, and regardless of telling her we can do it, it may take actually doing it day by day, rather than just talking the talk for her to believe it. I also don't want to tell her about my last relationship since that was, toward the end—a long-distance relationship that ultimately failed because of the distance.

But to be fair, the distance was across the entire country, from Seattle to Miami to be exact. I dated Marisa for three years, and when she got a job in Miami in the third year of our relationship, I swore that it would work, and we did make it work for a few months, until she stopped calling every night. Then every night turned into every few nights, and then once a week. When we dwindled down to every other week, until I went to her and we had a conversation that resulted my meeting her new boyfriend.

I was devastated and haven't really had a relationship since.

But in the long-run, I believe that she did us a favor. While I thought I loved her, I don't really think that I did. Sure, I liked her. I loved her in a way, but I didn't love her completely.

Do I love Peyton? It's too soon for me to even ask myself that question.

Can I see myself loving Peyton? I can indeed. And for that reason, I would like to see if we can try.

"I'm going to be honest with you, and that's because I believe that one of the fundamental parts of any relationship is honesty, my last relationship made me learn a lot."

Our arms are swinging playfully, and I notice the moment that it slows.

"What does that mean?" She swings her gaze in my direction.

"Well, we were great for the first two and half years, but the last few months were a little more difficult."

"Continue," she directs.

I want to put off on telling her all the details and I spot a cafe that is currently empty which would be perfect to divulge my biggest failure in.

I point in the direction, "want to grab a light dinner?" I ask.

"That would be great, less of a mess to clean up at your place," she nods.

We walk across the street and get a table right away. After we order, I place my arm on the back of her chair and pull her closer to me, so she's sitting beside me, rather than adjacent to me.

"I'm going to tell you about my last relationship, but I don't want you to try to search for any parallels to what we have." I say to her.

"This is kinda not what I was hoping for, should I be scared?" She asks.

"No, not scared, but definitely know that I had nothing to do with how the relationship ended," I tell her with full confidence.

She places her chin on her hand and leans toward me. "Okay, tell me everything," she says.

"I was in a relationship with someone for a few years, but then she got a new job. This job was out of state and she moved to

Miami. We worked well together for a few months before the communication dwindled. I did what I could to keep the relationship going, but she stopped communicating with me and then I found out that she ultimately was having another relationship with someone else. Someone that she met there not too long after she moved."

She gasps and covers her mouth. "How long before that happened?"

"I don't know. I never asked for details. But she started, about a month after she moved to slow down on the communications, despite how much I tried to talk to her."

"You wanted to make it work." Peyton says, more as a statement and to herself than a question.

"I did. Or at least I thought I did. I will admit that looking back now, I don't think I was fully in love with her. Otherwise, I would have offered to move for her when she did."

"How long ago was this relationship?" she asks.

"It was roughly five years ago." I reply with a shrug.

"Okay, go on," she prompts nodding as if taking note in her mind about the conversation.

"Well, I flew to Miami and she confided the reasoning for her lack of communication. She actually didn't need to tell me anything, as I came face to face with the man she was dating. So, we broke up, tried to keep things calm about it all and I came back here. I loved her, but I don't think that I was really in love with her."

"What does that mean?" she questions.

"It means that, yes, I loved her. But I wasn't in love with her. I wouldn't have done whatever it took to make sure that the end result of our relationship ended with the both of us together. I know there is nothing that could have been done, since she was romantically involved with someone else and was nothing that I had control over. It wasn't that I wasn't attentive, or that I was a bad boyfriend, but I know that if I was head over heels in love with her that I could have figured out a way to be together. I could have moved to Miami, but that was never a thought in my mind, or anything that I would have ever considered."

"But, you said something along those lines to me, that you would move to LA to be with me?" she questions.

"And I meant it."

CHAPTER THIRTEEN

"This one time in Vegas I almost got whiplash when the Magic Mike dancer whipped my chair around!"

PEYTON

And I meant it.

His words echo in my mind as I slip into bed tonight. I'm still sleeping in the guest room and a part of me feels guilty. Our relationship is progressing, we've kissed here and there, but up until this moment, I've been okay with taking it slow. However now, I'm anxious, eager, and I want more.

I sit up, remove the comforter from my body and with my hands on my knees, I take a deep breath. I push up to stand and shake out my arms to get rid of the jitters. I walk to the door of the bedroom and turn the knob.

He learned from his mistakes in previous relationship, and while I should be terrified that his long-distance relationship didn't work out, the way he worded it had proved he did every-thing in his power to try to make it work.

Even though I'm feeling a little self-conscious wearing only a shirt, I hold my head up and slip through the bedroom door, walking the short distance to his room. The door isn't closed, but open just a crack. The light illuminates part of the wall and I pause before breaching the space.

I hear the faint sound of the television, and hope that I'm not interrupting anything, like work. I take a deep breath and lightly knock on the open door.

"Max?" I say quietly, in case he doesn't hear the knock.

A moment later, the light expands into the hallway as he opens the door wider with his body filling the frame.

He's shirtless.

I fight every nerve of my body to touch his chest upon sight.

"Are you okay?" he asks with worry in his gaze as he looks me up and down to see if I'm injured.

My gaze meets his and I can tell the exact moment when he realizes what I'm standing in front of him for. I tentatively reach out and my fingertips dance across his skin, leaving goosebumps in the wake. Max takes a shaky breath in and releases it raggedly as if he's controlling himself.

I step into him, place my hands on his shoulders and lean up on my tiptoes. He meets me, and our lips tentatively brush against one another. His hand wraps around my waist and pulls me into him. With our bodies flush against one another, I pull on his bottom lip with my teeth, then sweep my tongue inside. The moment our tongues touch, electricity moves through my body.

Max growls in the back of his throat and deepens the kiss while walking us backward. When his legs hit the bed, I move with him as he sits down, and I straddle him—never breaking the kiss.

His arms hold me close to him then skate across my back

when my arms drape around his neck. I can feel his hardness under me and my hips instinctively grind into him.

"I want you," I say against his lips, arching my neck as his lips move down and splay across my skin.

"I've wanted you since day one," he replies against my skin.

He pulls away from the kiss for only a moment to grab the hem of my shirt and pull it over my head. His hands form to my breasts with his thumbs rubbing over my nipples, making the throbbing between my legs more prominent, my need heavier and the warmth throughout my body burn.

My body presses against his as we kiss with a heated passion that I've never experienced before. He leans back on the bed and I move with him with his hands floating to my hips, digging his fingertips into my flesh.

He flips me onto my back and looks down at me with a grin as he pushes hair behind my ear.

"I'm pretty nervous," he admits to me.

"We've done this before," I say with a laugh.

He shakes his head, leans down and bushes his lips across mine before leaning back up.

"Are you sure?" he asks.

"I've never been more sure of anything," I confess.

He reaches over me and rummages in a drawer beside his bed, pulling out a condom.

My fingers find the waistband of his sweats and I nudge them down. He leans up on the bed, giving me the perfect view of his body, and every second ticks by slowly as I wait for his sweatpants to come fully down while I pull my panties down and toss them on the floor beside the bed.

My mouth waters, my jaw drops, and my pulse begins to rise as his cock bobs out of its confinement. Max takes the condom and rips it open, sheathes himself quickly before leaning down and kissing me again as his hand creeps between us. His fingertips, tracing the softness between my legs, then tentatively plunging in.

I gasp at the feeling and lift my hips begging for more which he gives me right away.

"You feel so perfect, so wet," he says in a breath as he pulls his hand away, grabs his cock and slowly enters me.

My head pushes back into the pillow in pleasure, my mouth drops open with a silent moan as he thrusts into me, filling me to the hilt and satisfying me with every move.

MAXWELL

I bolt up in bed at the sound of my front door slamming and I hear a male voice echoing through my house that carries all the way to the bedroom. Peyton stirs beside me as I throw the covers off of me and get out of bed.

I put on my boxers and head towards the door cautiously.

There are only a handful of people who have the capability to get up to the Penthouse floor, but usually I have a heads up from either the front desk or the person themselves.

"What the fuck is happening here?" I ask when I see my friend, Jason looking in my fridge.

Jason whips around with a smile and spreads his arms as he teeters to the side.

"Maxi-boy!! How are you, man?" He smiles broadly.

I further walk into the kitchen until my hands rest on the counter and glare at them.

"What. Are. You. Doing. Here?" I look to the clock on the microwave, "at eight in the morning?"

"Just flew in and had nowhere else to go. My place isn't habitable right now," he says.

"Why not?" I ask.

"I decided to get the whole place renovated," he says with a nonchalant shrug.

"The whole damn place?" My jaw drops.

"I got bored and decided that I needed a change," he shrugs.

"Why didn't you call first, it's early and what if I wasn't here?" I ask.

"Well, I would have passed out in the guest room as I always do, unless you would have preferred that I snuggle with you instead. Do you need some extra loving?"

"What's going on?" Peyton walks up beside me rubbing the sleep out of her eyes at the worst moment.

Jason whistles and looks Peyton up and down.

"Who do we have here?" he asks, his interest perking up at her presence.

"Jason, this is Peyton, Peyton, my buddy Jason."

She gives an awkward wave as he just stares at her, as she pulls at her shirt.

"Wait a minute, you look familiar, do I know you?" he asks blinking several times.

"Um, no." she shakes her head, "I don't think so."

"Hold up! We met you in Vegas!" He points back and further between us, "you guys actually kept in touch? That's fucking rad! No one ever keeps in touch with their random hook up in Vegas. I speak from experience." He hiccups.

"Excuse him, he's a caveman." I say to Peyton with a roll of my eyes.

"I'm also still drunk and a little bit horny," he grins.

"There's nothing that we can do to help you with either." I turn to Peyton, "do you mind if I move your stuff out of the other room and let him sleep it off in there?"

"You guys aren't sleeping in the same room? What the fuck, man?" Jason asks eavesdropping.

"It's none of your business." I growl point at him as he steps back into the counter with his palm up.

"Shit! Okay. Well, I don't want to lick you out."

"You mean, 'kick', right?" I ask, anger bubbling within me.

"Huh? What did I say?" He asks in confusion.

"Lick," I reply through clenched teeth.

"Sorry, Freudian slip." he smirks.

Peyton grabs my arm and directs my attention to her. She leans up on her tiptoes and kisses my cheek.

"I'll move whatever is in that other room over to your room, you and Jason look like you are going to Gladiator this out, so I'll let you guys do that."

Peyton leaves as I stare down my oblivious friend.

"What?" He asks.

"You don't have to be a complete asshole, man."

"I'm not. I'm also really confused. What is she doing here?" He points after her.

"We're together. We're, um, actually married." I say quietly.

"Excuse me?" He says, "is she black-mailing you? What the fuck man, are you okay? Shit, we should have established code words for this shit. Blink once if you are being held against your will?"

"Shuddup. It's not like that. Also, I can't be held against my will in my own place."

"Bullshit. She's controlling you with pussy. I know how chicks operate."

I laugh. "You really need to sleep it off, and then we'll tell you everything."

Peyton comes in the kitchen. "The room is ready," she says with a smile.

"Is there a mint on my pillow?" Jason jokes.

"Fuck you man. Just go sleep it off, or I will punch you."

"Wow, getting laid sure does make you mean." Jason leaves the room quickly with a laugh down the hallway and closes the door behind him as he enters the room.

"I'm sorry about him. He's a good guy, I promise." I tell her.

"It's okay. My friends would do the same thing." She turns to me and wraps her arms around my neck. I bend to meet her halfway and cover her mouth with mine.

We kiss softly before pulling back. "Good morning." I tell her.

"Good morning. I have two more days here and then I have to go home," she reminds me.

"I know. I've been trying to not think about that." I lean down and kiss her again, she pulls away and smiles up at me.

"I want to be lazy with you."

"I'm not entirely sure what that means." I honestly tell her.

"I want to sit around the house with you, in our pajamas, not leave the place and watch television or do absolutely nothing. We can read, we can play board games, I don't know. But I think that will be fun, relaxing, and a good way to see if we're okay with not trying to impress one another."

"I will honestly say, that it's something that I've never done." I admit.

"You do have a television, right?" She asks.

I point over to the long table across from the couches that line the wall separating the living from the dining rooms. "The television comes up through the back of that table."

"Perfect. And do you have any board games?" She asks.

"I don't think so. I haven't had any board games since I was a kid." I shake my head.

"Well, that's the number one thing that we should do." She says excitedly.

"No, the number one thing that we should do is something while naked."

"Is that so?"

"Definitely." I lick my lips and grin. "I got a taste, and I want more."

CHAPTER FOURTEEN

PEYTON

Max leads me back to the bedroom with a tug of my hand and a grin that makes me weak in the knees. How I managed to not sex him up before last night escapes me. It was everything that I could have imagined and more.

I close the bedroom door and lock it behind us, just in case his annoying friend decides to sneak a peek when he shouldn't.

Max prowls to me as soon as he's in front of me, he reaches down and pulls my shirt over my head and tosses it on the floor. His fingertips lightly brush over my bare sides and I breathe in a shaky breath.

Max takes his time, gliding his hands across my skin,

worshiping my body as if he is memorizing every inch of my skin. When I'm standing in front of him completely naked, he lowers to his knees and leans in with his tongue lashing out at my center. I take a deep breath at the connection and feel my knees going weak.

With his hands on my bare hips, he guides me to the bed. My knees hit the back of the bed and I land on my ass softly with my hands holding me up. Max's body fits between my legs and leans up on the bed. He kisses my inner thigh and moves back to my center.

With a deep inhale, he moans.

"You smell delicious. I would sit here and take in your scent all day, if I could." He lashes his tongue and with his finger spreads me open while my body aches for him.

He laps me up, alternating between his tongue and his fingers. He pays attention to my clit while he fucks me with his fingers, his teeth lightly graze over my clit. With my toes curling, my hands gripping his bedsheet, I arch my back while my eyes clench and color blasts behind my eyelids as the pleasure takes over my body in the most explosive ways.

I was so into my orgasm that I didn't notice Max crawling up my body until his mouth meets mine and I taste myself on him, tracing my lips before plunging his tongue in.

Our tongues tangle and I feel his cock between my legs, nudging against my sex.

I want him.

I want him inside me, and I don't want him to ever stop.

"Condom," I say into the kiss.

He lays light kisses down my shoulder before pulling away. The weight of his body leaves mine and he walks around the bed and goes into the bedside drawer.

I move up on the bed as he takes off his boxers, unleashing a cock so beautiful that I could stare at it all day.

I lick my lips as his knee comes on the side of the bed. He sheathes himself quickly and fists his cock with smirk as he moves up and down his hardening length.

"Do you want it fast or slow, baby?" He asks as his head bends and he pulls a hardened nipple into his mouth.

"I want it in all the ways you want to give me," I tell him in a breath as I feel him again at my entrance.

"Can we have a lazy day, in bed?" He asks, the tip of his cock slowly entering me.

"Yes." I hiss as he pushes further into me until our bodies are flush against one another.

His forehead leans on my shoulder for a second, our hips move, and we become one.

With his hard body gliding over mine, I writhe underneath him. My hands moving back and forth between his back and fisting the bedsheets. Light moans come from my throat as heavy grunts come from him, the sounds bouncing off of the walls of his bedroom.

I cry out as I release unexpectedly, no build up, no warning signs, other than an eruption of pleasure. My moan is louder and deeper as I can feel my pussy clenching around him while he pistons into me. While my pleasure slows, Max doesn't. My hips meet him, thrust for thrust. I circle my hips from underneath which pulls a moan from him. I reach my hand between our bodies and find my clit. With the pad of my thumb, I lightly graze over it. Max notices the movement and leans up. He looks between our bodies as I push my button harder. I want to come again, I need to come again.

"I'm almost there," I whisper.

His eyes flick up to mine and he nods. He leans down and our lips touch for a moment, before he moves back up with his eyes on my fingers and his cock pushing in and out of me.

"I'm there, I need you to be there too." he says in between breaths.

"Now." I command.

His features tense as he pushes harder into me. My head hits the headboard and he pounds into me as his orgasm is releasing in time with mine. He pushes against me, deeply and then breathes a long sigh while his head drops, to my shoulder.

My hands move up and down his back, while our chests heave against one another.

"I don't want to move," he says against my skin.

He pulls out of me and rolls onto his back. His half hard cock landing on his thigh with his movements.

"I like this," he says turning his head to me.

"Yeah?" I ask.

"I do," he sits up and I watch the tight globes of his ass move while he walks into the bathroom. I hear the water running and he returns with a washcloth.

"Here, let me," he moves his hand between my legs and runs the warm cloth against my sensitive skin. He returns to the bathroom and climbs into the bed a moment later, pulling me tight against him.

"I wanted to wake up and do that to you, I'm sorry that there was a wrench thrown into the morning," he says.

"It's okay." I tell him.

"I want to do that every day, for the rest of my life." He declares.

"You're so sure, Mr. Addison."

"And you aren't, Mrs. Addison?"

MAXWELL

I think that the last time that I didn't do a thing was when I had my appendix taken out seven years ago. I was down for the count and forced to not go to the gym leave my placc or go into work.

That entire time, was unbearable. And from that boredom, I strive to always stay busy.

I know that you have to work hard, in order to play hard. Except that I forget to do the playing.

Peyton shows me what it is like to relax and take time to relish in life. We don't leave my place, we fuck as many times as I have condoms, and we ordered in food.

Jason emerged, looking ragged halfway through the day and made his apologies before leaving to stay at someone else's house leaving us alone. Allowing us to walk around the penthouse naked, to fuck on every surface, and to not have to worry about a damn thing.

"How is it that you've gotten to play hooky from work? I thought you were a workaholic?" Peyton asks laying on top of me, after another sensational round of sex on the couch.

"I have checked in here and there, but I took a few much needed vacation days. It was actually the first time that I've done so, that HR called me to make sure that I was okay," I laugh.

"I feel guilty when I take a day off. Like being here, has been both amazing and nerve-racking." she admits.

"Yet, you have done what your boss asked you to do. And I saw you on your email and Googling some vendors for one of the corporate clients." I tease poking her in the side.

"Since someone opened their mouth and said that they knew me, I feel like I would let down whatever glowing thoughts my boss has about me by knowing someone like you, if I did a whack-ass job." She defends.

"I'm pretty sure that you won't do a whack-ass job. Hell, I could even give you some heavy hitter names to make things easier?" *I know people in Los Angeles.*

"Don't you dare." She leans up and points at me.

Her bare breast peeking out between our bodies, making my mouth water and making me want her again.

Fuck, she's insatiable!

"I was just offering, might as well take advantage of me as much as you want now, I'm not going anywhere." I tell her.

"How are you so confident about this thing with us?" She asks.

"If it's something that I want, and I want you—I just feel confident in myself and the situation. It's how I'm wired. I have that in business and all the other areas in my life. Without that confidence, I don't think that I would be where I am today."

"But what if—"

"I don't deal with that, the 'what-ifs'. I seek out deals by looking at the companies, if I want it—I will get it. I will of course, work my ass to have it, and I see that not being any different with you. I will do what it takes to keep you. To have you as mine. Forever. Of course, should you allow it. How about you put that ring that I got you back on your finger?" I tell her with a grin.

"I wish I was like you." She lays her head on my chest, with my arms tightening around her as she ignores my request.

"We can't all be perfect," I laugh, as she playfully pinches my nipple.

Today Peyton goes back to Los Angeles and I go back to work. We start our first long distance week without seeing one another, aside from what technology will offer us. It's not what I want but it's what has to happen.

I stand at the trunk of my car and pull out her luggage, setting it down beside me. She walks around the passenger side of the car with a sad look on her beautiful face. She immediately wraps her arms around my middle and pushes her face into my chest. I feel her body lightly shake and after a moment, I come to the realization that she's crying.

"Hey, hey. What's this?" I as pulling her chin up.

"We've been together for two weeks and now we won't see each other," she sniffles and pulls back with her eyes red from the tears.

I wipe a falling tear from her eye. "We will both be so busy at work this week, that neither of us will notice how fast time goes, and then I'll be in Los Angeles Friday night," I remind her. "Time will go by fast."

"But right now, it feels so far away."

I pull her against me and kiss the top of her head, relishing in the touch and her presence.

"We can do it. Please, have faith. We've got this." I tell her.

She's quiet and I can feel the wetness on my shirt from her tears.

"Okay," she sniffles.

I rub her back and find it odd that I'm back in this type of relationship, a long-distance one, and I'm the one comforting again.

The Past

We're standing at the airport curb and Marisa is standing stoically with unshed tears in her eyes while standing in front of me.

"I can't believe this is happening right now, are you sure that you can't just move to Miami with me? That would make everything so much easier." She pouts.

"You know I can't do that. My work is here, there's nothing in Miami that I can do." I tell her.

"You can take the company there, I'm sure there are tons of companies that you can buy then sell, every city has the need."

Her tone is begging and slightly irritating. We've had this conversation before, and it plays out the same way each time.

"You know that's not possible," I tell her, more annoyed that we're having this conversation again than anything else.

She pouts, and I wrap my arms around her.

"You know that this isn't goodbye, that this is just a 'see you later' type of thing, right? Think of it as a business trip. We've done plenty of those and we've always been alright."

"Yeah, that's because we knew that we would be coming home to one another."

"Mare, listen. I love you and will be in Miami whenever I can, and then you will come back to Seattle whenever you can, we can do this."

"Yeah, I guess so." She wraps her arms around me and takes a deep breath.

"I'll be in Miami in a few weeks and in the meantime, we call each other every day."

"I'll be so busy anyways, that I won't have time for anything else when I first get there anyways," she says as if she's convincing herself of something.

"We got this." I tell her.

CHAPTER FIFTEEN

"This one time in Vegas, I went to celebrate my divorce with my friends. Four days later I was pushed through the airport in a wheelchair."

PEYTON

I've seen Max every day for the past two weeks, and today is the first day that I'm without him.

I miss him.

I didn't think that I would. And I've been so unbelieving that being with someone who doesn't live in the immediate vicinity could work, but here I am.

I miss him.

We're back to our daily schedules. I'll be at work, and so will he. But we will have a FaceTime call tonight as soon as he's home and so far, we've texted several times throughout the morning.

I woke up this morning with a text from him.

I got to work and had flowers on my desk from him.

And I had an email in my work inbox telling me to have a good day, from him.

He's thoughtful and making a point that he's in this relationship with his communication.

I'm sitting at my desk working on mock up invitations for the corporate event when Mr. Frederick walks into my office and sits down in front of my desk.

"I am torn over the place that we viewed in Seattle during the convention we went to, and the one that you saw and videoed me last week." He says immediately.

"Both places are beautiful, sir."

"Which do *you* like best?" He looks to me.

"I'm not sure, I think that they both have qualities that will be workable for a new office."

"Yes, but what one do *you* like?" he asks again.

"Why would my thoughts have any meaning in the plans for the new office?" I fold my hands in front of me.

"I trust your opinions. You run this office so efficiently that I believe your views are important. Since you've been here, you have helped turn us around and become more balanced between departments and as of recently with your personal connections, have brought us bigger clients."

"Well, I like the one that I saw this last week, if I'm being honest. It's closer in proximity to a lot of cafes and deep in the heart of downtown that you can immerse the business with a lot of other businesses that will hopefully keep word of mouth good. Plus, when I was doing the research, there isn't a business like ours in the immediate area." I tell him with confidence.

"Good, see that's the future thought of yours that I like. Do you have the contact information of the realtor? I would like to get in contact with them sooner rather than later?"

"Of course." I scoot my chair out and rummage through my purse for my wallet where I have the business card.

He looks it over and smiles. "Thank you, Peyton. I truly appreciate all your hard work." And leaves my office.

Why does he care what I think of the other office? It's not like he's going to transfer me to the new office.

Is he?

I'M LYING IN BED READING AN ARTICLE IN A MAGAZINE, WHEN MY phone lights up beside me. I sit up quickly and arrange my pillows behind me. I fluff up my hair and rub my lips together, hoping that I don't look too haggard after a long day.

I press the connect button and there's Max front and center on my screen.

His tie is loosened, and the top two buttons of his white dress shirt is undone. He has a little bit of a 5'o'clock shadow and the setting behind him is dark. His hair looks like his hands have ran through it repeatedly and from the bookshelves behind him, I can tell that he's not at home.

"Hi," I say with a smile.

"There you are, how are you?" he asks.

"I'm good, I'm good. Tired, work was busy, coming back from a week off, but time went by fast. How are you?" I ask.

"Still working, but I didn't want to keep you waiting."

"Are you still at work?" I ask.

"I'm taking a break from writing a proposal for a new takeover that I came across my desk today. I didn't want it to linger, and figured to get ahead of the game," he takes a deep breath. "But I don't want to talk about work."

"What do you want to talk about? It's been so long since I've actually had conversations on the phone, that I'm a little rusty."

"What did you do today?" he asks leaning back in his chair and putting his hands behind his head. His suit jacket is off and his biceps are stretching the fabric of his dress shirt.

"I thought you didn't want to talk about work?" I quirk my eyebrow.

"I don't want to talk about my work, it's boring. Parties are far more entertaining than company takeovers."

I laugh. "Whatever you say, my boss asked for my opinion about the Seattle offices and that was weird…" I trail off and tell him all the boring details of my day, as if we were together in person. After an hour of back and forth, I begin getting tired and he notices.

"I wish I was sitting in bed beside you, having you fall asleep in my arms," he says sweetly with a tilt of his head.

"Me too," I yawn while stretching out my arms to the side of me.

"Friday night. We made it through Monday, and we're that much closer," he says.

"I'm counting down," I tell him.

"Good. Me too. I'll let you get to sleep."

"You going to keep working?" I ask.

"I'll probably work for a little bit longer, then crash. I have a lot to get done this week that will make me free as a jailbird this weekend, so I want to make sure I'm not working at all this weekend with you."

"It's okay if you have to, you know. You don't need to go silent, it's work, and it's important."

"And so are you. Get some rest, I'll talk to you tomorrow."

"Aye, aye Captain." I salute him playfully.

"Oh, the ideas, night babe." he smiles.

"Night."

We hang up and I drift off to sleep with his face in my mind, and a smile on my face.

MAXWELL

"You won't believe this, but this fool right here, is fucking married!" Jason hooks a thumb in my direction as he announces the news to the table.

Grayson, Jason, Marcus and I were enjoying our weekly Thursday night out for beers and burgers when Jason decided to announce the news. "We need to call Devin and clue him into this, he'd shit his pants!" Jason pulls out his phone, but I push it away.

Grayson nearly chokes on his food and Marcus began coughing after taking a sip of his beer.

"You? Mr., I have no time for anything fun Addison is married? Who did you knock up?" Marcus asks.

"No one," I wave off. "Leave Devin alone, he hates it when we call him as a group, he doesn't have the patience for group calls. I'll call him on my own."

"So, when did you get married and where were we?" Grayson asks.

"Get this, it's the chick that we partied with at the club in Vegas!" Jason chimes in.

"You married a stripper?" Marcus asks, his eyes wide.

"No." I shake my head. "Wait, we hung out with strippers?"

"I think so, we did a lot that weekend. But wait, seriously, you got married? To who?" Grayson asks.

"Her name is Peyton. Long story short, I didn't remember anything when I woke up. She wasn't there, but I had flashbacks about a chick and a wild night. I hired a PI and he returned with the info that I got hitched."

"So, get an annulment."

"Well, I had every intention of doing so. But then I went to Los Angeles and met her. Or actually re-met her."

"And now, they're in love. It's gross. I met her last week and they were making googly lovey dove eyes at each other." Jason interrupts.

"What? Is that why we didn't see you last week?" Marcus asks.

"So, you're not going to get it reversed? You're going to stay married to this woman?" Grayson asks.

"I like her. A lot." I shrug.

"She lives in Los Angeles, man. Remember what happened the last time you were in a long-distance relationship?"

"Yeah, but I think I've grown up a bit. Listen, we're getting to know one another, and I'm pretty happy with how things are going. So, yeah, we're staying married and hoping that it works out." I shrug. "We're being casual about the relationship and feeling things out to see if it could be a legit thing."

"Who are you and what did you do with our friend?" Grayson shakes his head.

"I guess my bachelor party in Vegas was more for you than for me. Congrats man." Marcus holds up his beer. "Let's be happy for Max, he might finally learn that life has more in it than business." Everyone clinks their glasses together and we divert subjects again.

I pull out my phone and smile at the random text on my screen from Peyton.

Peyton: True or False: Max's favorite fruit is strawberries.

Me: False. It's a toss-up of tomatoes and avocados. I could eat avocados for days and I will eat a tomato like one does an apple.

Me: This or That: Warm sunny beach or fireside in a snow cabin?

Peyton: Warm sunny beach. I prefer sand between my toes and it's not recommended to be barefoot in snow.

Me: Yeah, that's probably not a very good idea.

"What are you smiling about over there, lover boy?" Jason teases.

"Nothing," I say pocketing my phone.

"He's texting with his wife. Making sure that you don't have to be home by a certain time?" Marcus laughs.

I LIKE COMING HOME AND IMMEDIATELY TALKING TO PEYTON. ON my way home, I phone her while I drive, and while I couldn't see her, I have her voice throughout the car.

Talking to her is easy, but I want to touch her too.

One more day.

We just have to wait one more day before we can see one another again.

I wake up the next morning to the lobby phone ringing. I shuffle across my space and answer it with a yawn.

"Sir, there is a delivery here for you. I wanted to assure that you were home, prior to sending it up."

"A delivery? This early?" I look at the clock on the wall. It's six in the morning and I will kill the person who is waking me up thirty minutes before I'm supposed to be up.

My doorbell rings and I stomp over to the door, one of the front desk attendants is smiling and holds out a basket. I take it, quietly thank her and then close the door with my foot.

I place the basket on the kitchen island and unfold the covering to at least a dozen muffins.

My mouth waters on sight and my annoyance dissipates.

There's only one person right now that would send me something like this. I head into the bedroom and grab my tablet. I want to see her on a bigger screen, rather than my small phone.

I prop the tablet up and press to dial her.

She answers with her hair wrapped in a towel and wearing a tank top. Her bedroom is in the background.

"Did I catch you at a bad time?" I ask.

"Not at all. I was actually expecting a call or a text from you. Good morning." She smiles.

"Are these delicious things, your crafty work?" I ask holding up a still warm muffin.

"They may be," she smiles proudly. "I went to this amazing bakery that was right by your place and the muffins were to die for. And I know you like a good pastry. I wanted you to start your morning off right."

"I vote to start my morning with you every morning, I think we need to add mornings to our phone schedule."

She moves around her room and places the phone on her dresser. She bends and moves the towel over her hair and flips back up.

"I hope you don't mind me getting ready while we're on?" She asks looking at the phone.

"I will have no objections, especially since you will have to get dressed and I'm hoping that I get to watch that too." I grin before taking a bite out of the muffin. I moan at the taste. "Holy crap, this is delicious." I hold up the muffin as she laughs.

This is something that I want every day; breakfast and laughs with my wife.

My wife.

CHAPTER SIXTEEN

"This one time in Vegas, I got a handjob from a stripper, and I forgot to tip her."

PEYTON

I'm sitting in my living room right now as he showers. He tried to talk me into showering with him, but after the marathon of bedroom activities since getting here last night, I think a small break is in order.

He's insatiable. And the sex just keeps getting better and better.

Everything does. Our relationship. The sex. The communication. Every part.

The weekends that Max is in LA, Quinn disappears to give us some space, aside from the times that we've gone out with my friends. When we're in Seattle, we've made it a point to do something with his friends as well, and so far, we've all gotten along.

The water shuts off and shortly after, the bathroom door opens.

"Babe?" He calls.

"I'm in the living room," I return.

A moment later, he comes out of the hallway and my mouth waters at the sight of him.

Ripped taunt skin stretching over his still wet body, his hair is slicked back and he has the stubble that I've begged him to keep on the weekends, he stands in his towel in front of me.

"What, did you think I left?" I laugh.

"No, I was just hoping that you would be lying naked on your bed when I got out," he winks.

"You're incorrigible. I was thinking that we could go grab some breakfast?" I ask.

"I'm hungry for something else," he prowls toward me. I stand up quickly and dart out of his reach and around him. "Oh no, you don't." He growls.

I run into the bathroom and lock the door behind me, giggling with my back against the door.

"You aren't going to get away with this," he says on the other side of the door.

"You can get me later on tonight. I'm so hungry and I want pancakes!" I say in between giggles and breaths.

I push off the door and get in the shower a moment later.

When I come out of the bathroom, Max is laying on my bed, still in his towel on his back with his arms behind his head and his legs crossed at his feet.

He wiggles his eyebrows at me.

"Pancakes." I say.

"Can you blame me for wanting you?" He asks.

"I don't, really I don't. But we need to go to the store after pancakes and get more condoms anyways. We've depleted my supply."

He sighs audibly and sits up.

"You win, if I had it my way, I'd have you bent over your bed, you realize that, right? But I love you too much to postpone you from your pancakes."

"Wait, what? What did you say?" I freeze in front of my dresser and turn to him in shock.

"Oh, well, I imagine that's not exactly the way one would want to hear that. Shit, okay. Pretend I said nothing," he backpedals.

"You put love and pancakes in the same sentence. You said... you... love... me?" I stutter, feeling my bottom lip tremble.

He stands up, still in his towel and places his arms on my arms while looking at me tenderly.

"I do. I love you, Peyton. I think that I have been in love with you from the start. When I stood in your living room, when I came here to see you."

"You love me." I repeat.

"I love you." He says again.

"Wow." I say, looking up to him "Max?"

"Yeah?"

"I love you too." I drape my arms around him and pull him down for a kiss. Both of our towels fall to the ground moments later and with my heart beating so loud I can hear it, we fall to the mattress.

His body covers mine as our mouths crash and we devour one another. With our bodies in line together as he gently nudges his cock into my pussy. We pull apart and stop moving as we realize that he's inside me without a condom.

Both of us are breathing heavily with the intensity of emotions that we're both feeling.

His hand brushes hair out of my eyesight and he smiles.

"I'm sorry, just give me a second. If I pull out of you too fast right now, I may blow it, and—"

"I want you to keep going." I tell him.

"But I'm not wearing a condom."

"I'm clean, I'm on birth control, you're the only person that I'm with, that I want to be with," I say.

"Same. I mean, everything except for the birth control."

"Make love to me, Max." I ask.

Our hips glide together slowly, as we pour our emotions into the kiss into the single most erotic moment of our relationship so far.

MAXWELL

I didn't intend to tell Peyton that I was in love with her in the way that I did, but it came out naturally.

Saying those words to one another, while as sappy as it sounds, brought us closer and this trip will go down in the books as the most memorable of the past few months.

It's the trip where my girlfriend, my wife told me that she loves me.

After celebrating our declarations to one another, I took her out for pancakes and watched her devour and love every single bite.

"I want to run something by you," she starts with full mouth.

"Sure thing, what's up?" I reply popping a piece of bacon in my mouth.

"Now, this has nothing to do with the events of this morning. But my boss has been hinting at a few things over the past few months."

"Oh, yeah? What's this?" I quirk an eyebrow in curiosity.

"So, you know how I told you that my boss was asking for my opinion on the Seattle office, right?"

"Yeah," I say leaning into her.

"So, what if I volunteered to be transferred over to the new office? The one in Seattle?"

"Is that an option?" My interest is peaked.

"I'm not sure what his plan is completely, but he keeps coming to me for all things related to the new office. I've been in a few meetings about the new space, and even though, he hasn't said it outright, I think that if I even suggest that I make the transfer he will immediately approve it. I think he's just waiting for me to catch on," she smiles.

"And you have caught on." I state.

"I have." She nods.

"Well, what are you waiting for?" I ask, "call your boss right now and make the offer!" I smile.

"Chill out, there's a lot more to talk about before making a huge decision like that. Plus, it needs to be known right from the start, that while yes, I do love you—gosh, that sounds so liberating saying out loud—that I would be moving for work and not for you. I would also need to talk to Quinn, since that would mean I would have to move out and she would be responsible for my half of the rent."

"You make that sound so horrible, like it's a bad thing that you would be moving for me." I say jokingly.

"Well, that's a bonus." She says with a lift of her shoulder. "But I wouldn't be moving just for that, I'm not that kind of girl. It's a big decision, and I would still need to weigh all the options. But it's an option."

"I would have no objections if you choose to do that." I reply.

I wasn't sure if we were there yet. If we were at the point where we would determine who would move to be with one another. But I'm definitely lying to myself as I have been looking into options for the past month. Opening an office in another state wouldn't be an overnight thing, but it appears that Peyton's boss put his gears into motion faster than I did.

"It's not pathetic?" She looks to me for assurance.

"Why would it be pathetic? Your boss is actually opening an office in my city. That was something that was in the works before I tracked you down." I tell her.

"I guess that's true." She smiles taking another bite of her stack. "I will talk to my boss on Monday, gauge where he is and then we'll see. More conversation to come, but I just wanted to see if this would be an okay thing."

I stand up and scoot her over on her side of the booth, place my arm around her and pull her to me.

"Babe, this is the most okay thing that I've ever discussed. I told you that I want to have my mornings and nights with you, this is just a more legit way of getting it to happen instead of kidnapping you."

"Kidnapping? You wouldn't dare!"

"Don't you know that the first road trip, up to Seattle was my first attempt?" I joke.

"Yet, you still let me go," she teases right back.

"That's a part of my charm." I wink.

"You're horrible."

"Want to adventure today?" I ask.

"You... adventure?" She quirks an eyebrow as if she doesn't believe me.

"Humor me."

We leave the diner and I get behind the wheel of her car. I use the address in my email and find parking at the bottom of the hill of the parking lot.

"What are we doing here?" she asks.

We're walking up the hill to head to the Griffith Observatory, something that I've always wanted to do. A location that you see countless times in movies and I've wanted to see it for myself.

"I've never been here before," I tell her. "I thought that it would be a fun thing to do. Have you ever been here before?"

"No," she shakes her head.

I grab her hand and we make our way up towards the top of the hill. We stop at a bench halfway up with a view of the Hollywood sign and we rest on the bench for a minute.

"I never really looked at Los Angeles as being anything other than a concrete jungle. I didn't think that all of this was really lush in greenery." I say to her.

"There's a whole other world here, you just need to know where to go. There's canyons, there's trails and it's not too far for the forest. We have mountains and then we have the beach," she explains. "Then there's the other end, the freeways and the roads. That's what you would call the concrete jungle. But it's all about finding the level of what you want."

"And what level of the world, do you normally look for?" I ask.

"A mixture. I don't do the hiking thing, but I like to get outdoors whenever I can. I work downtown, so I have a lot of concrete in my life on a regular basis."

"True, but you have the options for all of it, right?"

"I do. Sometimes, work takes me out of the office and to nice venues outside of downtown. But when I'm driving, it's alright because I get to listen to my podcasts or my music."

"That doesn't sound like a bad thing," I take a deep breath, look up the hill, and then return to her. "Are you ready to get to the top?" I ask her as I stand and offer her my hand.

WE DID LOS ANGELES TOURIST THINGS WHILE IN THE CITY AND later that night ordered Chinese food. I've gone from the constant working and never having a moment that wasn't focused around work to lounging around with a girlfriend and eating takeout without looking at or touching my phone. Enjoying my time and not rushing through it.

Sunday night came too fast and I was boarding a red eye plane back home, hoping that this is one of the last times that I would have to.

I go to sleep upon getting home, with the thoughts of how different my future could be, all because of a night that happened in Vegas.

CHAPTER SEVENTEEN

"This one time in Vegas, I tried to get married, but both 24-hour license offices were closed, telling me to go to the other. "

PEYTON

I knock lightly on my boss's door the day after my visit with Max ended.

He looks up and smiles immediately which normally puts me at ease, except today, my nerves are sky-high and I'm pretty sure there's sweat dripping down my spine.

"How are you?" he asks sitting back in his chair.

"I'm good, I'm good. I have something that I wanted to run by you, do you have a moment?" I step further into his office.

"Of course. I always have time." He motions to the chair across from him, "what's on your mind today?"

"Well, I was doing some thinking about the Seattle office, and I was thinking that maybe it would be a good move, for me."

"Do you think that you can elaborate here?" he asks.

"I was thinking that maybe I can take a lead role in the new office?"

A large smile forms on his face and then he claps startling me.

"At last! I have been waiting for you to make it your idea."

"Excuse me?" I ask.

"I've told you before, you've turned this office around and have made our client base even more provocative to new customers as well as being the sole reason that our offices would expand."

"So, the looking at property and asking my opinion was a plan to get me out of here?" I ask in shock.

"The office is yours, you can be managing director if you choose to make the move. We would of course pay for lodging for three months and I would of course have Marjorie in Human Resources come and assist with the hiring process for staffing. I, of course would be in and out of town as well, I wouldn't leave you completely alone."

"Okay, wow. Um, I really wasn't expecting this to be the actual plan. When would you like to have the open date on the new office?" I ask.

"I'm looking for a three month turn around; would that be enough time?" He asks.

My mind is reeling. Is it enough time? Can I do this? Am I jumping into this too soon?

"I think so," I stutter with self-doubt creeping in.

"You're looking a little nauseous, are you okay?"

"I didn't come in here thinking that this would actually happen. I had hoped so, because it sounds like a great opportunity, but I wasn't thinking that it was something you were already planning."

"Do you need to take more time to think about it?" He asks with concern.

Now that's it's all been said out loud, the offer and the expectation—everything just became a little more, no a lot more real and I'm freaking out. The potential plan of moving to Seattle is now extremely real, and not just talk, which makes all my emotions rush forward.

"I think I'm going to throw up." I cover my mouth, stand and rush to the wastebasket just to the side of where I'm sitting. With one hand on the wall steadying me, I put my other hand on my forehead and take some deep breaths.

I'm getting dizzy at the thought of everything happening so fast.

"Peyton are you okay?" Mr. Frederick stands up and rounds his desk. He places his hand on my shoulder and looks at me.

"I'm good, I'm good. I should though probably think about it a little more. First it was an idea, now it's an offer and oh boy, I wasn't really expecting this to become real when it was said out loud." I ramble.

"I want you to work from home today, think about it. It's a huge decision, one that moves you from one city to another. I want you to do your pros and cons list, to really figure out whether or not this is something that you want and can do." He says, "I have no doubt that you can handle this, but I want you to be one hundred percent sure."

I nod and with a pat on the back, I leave his office and gather my things. I'm still freaking out. While I was completely sure that this was something that I could do, now I'm second guessing myself.

Now, I'm panicking.

Moving to Seattle would mean that I leave everything that I know. I haven't lived anywhere outside of California before and while, yes, I would have Max—my friends are here.

I don't remember driving back to Echo Park and walking in the front door. Quinn looks confused as I walk in the door and wouldn't leave me alone until I asked her to call Hanna and tell her to come over.

Quinn looks terrified but did as I asked. She sat by my side in silence and as soon as there was a knock on our door, she jumps up quickly and a moment later, I have my two best friends on both my sides with worried looks.

"Are you pregnant?" Quinn asks.

"Did you guys break up?" Hanna asks.

I look between them. "No." I say simply to both questions.

"Then what the hell is going on, you are worrying us to high hell!" Quinn says.

"I've got to talk to you guys about something, I need your help, your insight and advice."

MAXWELL

I know that Peyton was going to talk to her boss today, and it's got me on pins and needles. We exchanged our normal cheery texts in the morning, but I haven't heard from her since and I'm also not completely sure when in her day she would be speaking to him, or even what he would say.

My hopes, of course are that this means within a short period of time, we would be living in the same city.

When I didn't hear from her at all through the day, I tried to call her before I walked into the bar to meet the guys. When I couldn't get through to her, I sent her a text.

Me: Is everything okay? I've tried to call you and haven't heard from you all day.

I don't see the dancing dots, I don't see that the message has been read, maybe she's just busy or driving, who knows.

I walk into the bar and see that the guys are already seated and talking up a storm. I unbutton my blazer and slide into the booth to jump right into the conversation to get my mind off of the woman who I can't stop thinking about.

The night is full of banter and drinking, with no response back from Peyton. Concern is in the back of my head, but being over a thousand miles away, prevents me from being able to take initiative aside from driving or flying to LA myself. I'm not going to jump to conclusions and I'm not going to push my way in, just in case I am overreacting.

As soon as I get home, I try to FaceTime with her, but the call still gets unanswered. I check back with my text and that message hasn't been read yet either.

I look down at Scout, laying with his head on my thigh. He looks up to me, as if knowing I'm worried about something. I pet him and give him a smile, though I don't feel the smile.

What is happening? Is there something wrong?

CHAPTER EIGHTEEN

"This one time I was in Vegas, I thought wow the strip is smaller, than I thought it would be. I realized I was in Reno the next morning."

PEYTON

I've been putting off on talking to Max for two days. He's texted, he's called and I have controlled myself when his name would show up to not touch my phone. I don't want to give him bad news and I've been trying like hell to come to some sort of crossroads in what my future plan is.

I ran through everything that has been said to all parties within the past few days. When talking to Hanna and Quinn, they were attentive with listening and then let me in on their thoughts and that's when I realized that I made a mistake.

They were hurt.

They were mad.

And most of all, they felt that our friendship came last.

That's a feeling that I have never wanted anyone to think.

They are concerned with why I haven't spoken to them about any of this, when it was more of a beginning thought versus an actual offer and plan.

So, we sat on the couch, with me in the middle for over an hour as I explained to them what has been going on.

Neither of them thought that the relationship with Max was that serious, serious enough to move out of state for. And neither of them had any clue about the expansion of the company.

I've been a shitty friend and I'm not sure if it's because I've been so wrapped up with Max or if I've just become so selfish that I let everything else slip through my fingers in ignorance.

"I thought that you were just going to have your fun with the hot guy in the suit and then be done with it, get that divorce and shit?" Hanna asked.

"I thought so too, at first. But then things became real. We became more and more real, and in turn—I fell for him." I shrugged.

"Are you in love with him, Pey?" Quinn questioned.

I nod my head. I do. We told one another that we did, was that too fast?

Shit, I was, or I am planning to move to Seattle, and the added benefit is that Maxwell lives there.

Am I being blinded by lust or am I trying to advance my career by taking the job my boss is offering me?

WHAT DO I DO?

What am I doing?

I checked in with my boss and let him know that I'm still thinking about the details of the offer and he even offered to give me the rest of the week to decide. I've taken half of the week to mull over the pros and cons, only to start to feel more and more stressed based off of talking with my friends.

I've dodged phone calls from Max and in return would text him back that I'm not feeling well.

Which made me feel even more guilty when he sent me flowers and had Grub-hub deliver soup to the apartment. I sent him texts, that were short and didn't hold much of a conversation, all because my mind was fucking with me and I wasn't sure that I was making this decision because of him or not.

But after a full week of not talking to him, a lot of pulling my hair and my subconscious taking over for me, I came to my final decision.

I was nervous, but I knew that I needed to give my boss an answer. I waited long enough. And then after I talk to him, I will have to put on my big girl panties and talk to Max.

I walk into work and settle into my office. I go about my usual start-up of my day and keep my eye on the clock, waiting for Mr. Frederick to come in.

Busy work and catching up keeps me occupied as well as makes me lose track of time.

Mr. Frederick steps into my office and sits down in the chair in front of me, while I'm putting the finishing touches on the invoicing for the week and places a coffee in front of me.

I look up surprised, then look at the time.

"Oh God, time got away from me," I say.

"That's what happens playing catch up," he smirks.

"I was going to come and find you when you normally get in, but I got distracted with work."

"I guess that's a good thing to be distracted with, how are you?" he asks.

"Well sir, to be truthful, my stomach has been in knots all week."

"Is this about the offer?" He quirks an eyebrow.

"It is," I pause. "Maybe we should shut the door."

He stands up and closes the door to my office and then turns around with anticipation.

MAXWELL

More radio silence.

I'm not used to a woman going radio silent on me. Truthfully, it's usually the other way around. I'm the guy who doesn't call back or doesn't make a second date. I avoid phone calls and texts, because that's who I have been since Marisa.

I haven't been the relationship guy in several years, and right now, I'm wanting to be and give this thing between us a real shot —but I'm afraid that she's icing me out.

She says that she's sick, but a part of me is worried that she is completely avoiding me.

I'm concerned that she's not being completely honest with whatever she's dealing with and I fear that it has to do with her moving here or even potentially with our relationship. Even with her silence, I've still discussed with the board and had a new office location approved. I've virtually toured spaces in Los Angeles and put a bid on two properties after a friend of mine in the area having vouched for it.

When discussing with the board my plans, they mentioned that the market was currently good and agreed with me that our name brand would benefit in expanding down the coast.

While I know that the marriage happened on a drunken night, I feel that the time we've spent getting to know one another, has been perfect. We complement one another and for that, it gives me hope that this relationship, this marriage could really last.

My phone on my desk buzzes and I turn it over, nearly fall out of my chair in excitement, but straighten to play it cool when I answer the call.

I clear my throat, pull my collar from my skin and put a smile on my face as I swipe across to receive her call.

"Peyton." I say.

"Hi Max," she says quietly.

I look at the time and notice that it's still mid-day.

"How are you? Are you feeling better?" I ask with concern.

"Do you have a minute to talk? Am I interrupting anything?" she asks, her voice sounding off.

"I have all the time in the world for you. Is everything okay?"

I hear her rummage around in the background and then the sound of a door closing.

Where is she?

Is she home? Work?

I scratch my head and wait for her to talk.

"I don't think that I can do this anymore," she drops.

"Say that again?"

CHAPTER NINETEEN

"This one time in Vegas, I was walking through a casino in the middle of the day when a "pretty, young thing" asked if I would like company. Immediately, a woman in a suit and a big guy in a security uniform intercepted us. The suit said with a smile to my companion, 'You know that you're not supposed to be in here at this time of day'"

PEYTON

I told him that I can't do this anymore.

I said it was the distance and that I would be unable to make the move, that now wasn't the right time.

I said that we rushed into a relationship and that everything was moving too fast.

I told him I needed time.

I could tell that he wasn't expecting this type of conversation, because of that, I tried to keep it as short and to the point as much as possible.

It killed me.

I had fallen hard for him. I loved him. No, I love him.

But my friends were right. I let the emotions guide me and I just ran with it.

I let the feeling of being with him, consume me, and that's just not who I am. I let my heart guide me and not my mind. I don't want to be the girl to move somewhere for a guy. It's not that he's not worth it, but I just can't regardless of how much I care for him. Am I him when his ex moved to Miami?

With my boss giving me the opportunity to lead a whole new office, that would be a great opportunity, but I love my job as it is. I don't want to be an actual manager. I can't handle the responsibility that could entail. At least not right now in my life. Perhaps, down the road.

And while I turned down his offer, he understood.

Then, the call to Max.

That was harder than I thought it would be.

Did I make the wrong decision? Should I have moved to Seattle, taken the job and followed my heart? It's too late now, I made my choice, broke up with him and I can't go back on it. He's likely moved on by now, and I just have to accept that I likely ruined the single most important relationship that I've ever had.

I fought crying until now, and here I sit, beside Quinn with a bowl of ice cream, wrapped in a blanket.

She goes through the channels and settles on an episode of a reality show.

"This will be good nonsense to watch, I think that most reality shows lack the substance to really get involved with too much, the plot is pretty basic." She turns her head towards me and offers me a smile.

"Sounds good to me," I say, my voice lacking emotion before I shovel another spoonful of Chunky Monkey in my mouth.

I'm not sure how long we sit there, but after several episodes and two-bathroom breaks, I'm ready to crawl into my bed.

I haven't touched my phone since ending the call with Max, but I'm tempted to check it, to see if he left me any messages.

I decide against checking my phone and instead head straight to bed.

"PEYTON!" QUINN CALLS FROM THE OTHER SIDE OF THE DOOR. "Peyton! You need to get up or else you'll be late to work; don't you have that event tonight?"

I bolt up in bed and throw the covers off of me as I stumble around my bedroom in a haze.

In the past two weeks, I've busted ass at work to stay busy and not think about Max. I've lived and breathed the projects that I have going on, and that includes the event that Max may have thrown my name into the hat for. My nights have involved copious amounts of ice cream and trash TV that I'm pretty sure that I've done a good mixture of keeping occupied.

The event is tonight, and my nerves are skyrocketed.

Would he be there?

I haven't heard from him since I broke up with him over the phone. I managed to file for the divorce that we should have gotten from the beginning and send him off the paperwork.

Who were we kidding?

That wasn't a relationship that would last.

That was a fun fling, spurred by a wild night in Vegas.

I ran across the hall, in to the bathroom and in impeccable timing, was out the door ten minutes later, looking as if I hadn't slept through my alarm and also looking like a million bucks in an emerald pencil skirt and white blouse.

I walk briskly into the building and past all the cubicles to my office.

I pick up all the paperwork for the event and begin with making the calls to put everything into place.

Halfway through the day, I have my clipboard, a headset and all my notes. My assistant for the event has yet to show up.

The event begins, and I do my best to keep to the outskirts of the party. I observe and where appropriate, I make sure items get replenished. Towards the end of the night, my boss approaches me with a smile on his face and a relaxed gait.

"This is a remarkable event, I'm very proud of the work that you've done here," he gently elbows me.

"Thank you, sir. I enjoyed all of the ins and outs of what corporate events entail, it's been a good learning process. A lot different from how the private personal parties are, that's for sure," I reply.

"Are you sure that you want to pass on the Seattle office? Maybe take it over temporarily? I think your work here has been outstanding. You have a keen eye for the details and the clients are very happy."

"I think I would need a lot more experience, sir. With all due respect, I think that I would need a lot more event experience under my belt. While I know how to run the office, I think there is still so much more that I can learn there."

"You are remarkable, and I applaud how much thought you've put into my offer," he commends.

"Thank you." I blush and look down at my clipboard to distract myself.

For the remainder of the night, I walk around the outskirts of the event, observing the interactions between guests, the decorations and the food. I sign off with vendors and eventually make my way to my car in the parking garage underneath the building after a final walk through to make my way home.

I collapse into bed immediately, my body melts into the mattress with my eyes shutting upon contact and the world going dark.

Another day down, another day without Max.

Something that I need to get used to.

He was too good for me anyways.

MAXWELL

I can't freaking believe it!

How have things come to this?

I guess the typical progression to the end of a marriage would be for a divorce, but I would have spoken to her if that was the path I had chosen. I admit I hadn't been upfront with her and that she's not aware of what I've been doing on my end about the new office location.

She doesn't know how close I am to closing on a deal, and she sure as hell isn't aware of what I'm willing to do for her, despite my saying it when we first met and over several conversations.

Why am I willing to move mountains to be with Peyton, when I wasn't even close to doing anything of the sort for Marisa?

What is it about her that makes her different from anyone else?

Is it because she clearly doesn't need me?

Does that make me need her more?

Or is it because I finally understand what love is?

I shake my head and continue with stuffing a few shirts into my duffel bag. I don't plan to take much, after all, I will need to come back in a week to downsize and sign paperwork for the condo. But I need to finalize the deal on the new property, and I want to do that in person for more than one reason.

I look around my bedroom, wondering if I've left anything that I need behind, then figure to wing it. If I need anything, then I can buy it.

I have places to be. And a woman to win over.

―――――――

NERVES RATTLE AS I PUT MY CAR IN PARK IN FRONT OF HER apartment building. I haven't seen her in almost a month, and every single day has sucked. But now, I'm sitting outside of her house and my body is pulsing with the need, knowing that she is so close.

I sit in my car longer than I need to be, my palms are sweating and my knee jumping with the nerves that I have with the anticipation of seeing her. I drove straight here and through the night, anxious to see her and anxious to be at my final destination. I likely look a mess, but there's not time to freshen up, when I just want to get this part of my life back on track.

Every few minutes, I glance up at her building.

It's a normal complex, brown in color and just a block building with rails and doors leading to the inside. Nothing about the complex screams to stick out, but to me it does, because of who is inside.

My woman.

My wife.

With that last thought, I get out of the car and round to the trunk, grab my duffel bag and head towards her stairwell to her door on the second floor.

I let my feet guide me up the stairs and to her door.

Standing in front of it, my mind wanders, and I hesitate.

Recalling the day that I stood in this very same place, with the nerves months ago. How things are different now.

What if she doesn't want me anymore?

What if her divorce filing was what she wanted and I have no chance?

I raise my hand and knock on her front door, eagerly waiting for her to answer the door.

When the door swings open, I'm standing there, speechless as I take in her beauty.

She looks absolutely breathtaking and comfortable in her pajamas with her hair up and it's as if I haven't seen her in months, when it's only been weeks. Not one part of me feels like backing down. I will fight for this woman, and I will prove to her just how much that I love her.

I love her.

I really do love her.

CHAPTER TWENTY

"This one time in Vegas, I was at   the Bellagio when someone tried to rob it."

PEYTON

The knock on the door in the middle of a Saturday afternoon surprises me. It's not often that we have people knocking on our doors, unless one of us can't find the keys.

But, Quinn is passed out, likely hungover from last night in her room. And I'm lounging around in my flannel pajamas watching *The Greatest Showman.*

I open the door, wary of who is on the other side and once I see him, my heart begins to pound.

He looks like he hasn't shaved in a few days, with dark circles under his eyes and his clothes are wrinkled. He has a bag thrown over his shoulder and gives me an exhausted smile as I open the door fully.

"Hi," I say, unsure of how else to greet him.

"Hey," he replies, shifting his weight from one foot to the next.

"What are you doing here, in LA?" I ask. I look to his feet and Scout is sitting patiently, wagging his tail, waiting to be acknowledged. "Hey Boy," I smile before returning my gaze to Max.

"Well, I'm here for you. For us."

I blink, unsure of what he's talking about.

"What do you mean?"

"Can I come in?" he asks. "Can, we come in?" he motions to the dog as well.

I move aside and he walks past me, with Scout trailing behind him. Even though, he looks crumpled, I smell his familiar scent and my memory comes back with the yearning to touch him.

I refrain, and watch as he moves to the couch to sit down, and sets his bag on the floor, with scout turning in circles before settling beside his feet like a trusty companion. I sit at the opposite end of the couch and wait for him to start explaining why he's here.

"Max?" I prompt him after a few minutes of uncomfortable silence.

"I love you," he blurts out.

When I open my mouth, he holds up his hand and continues on.

"I love you and I am not going to let you go as easily," he digs into the bag beside his feet and pulls out a large envelope to toss between us, "I'm not willing to sign the divorce papers, because I am in love with you and want to make us work. I will do anything to make us work."

"Max," I begin. "I told you that I can't move."

"That's why I'm moving here. A month or two ago, I put into motion the plans to open an office here in Los Angeles. In fact, I will be signing the paperwork this week, to add the final touches on the contract for the lease and to begin holding interviews for staffing."

I shake my head, as if there's water in my ear that is making me hear things.

"What?" I ask.

"I knew from the moment that we met, sober," he winks, "that you would be the endgame for me. I want to be with you, here, where you are, and make a life for ourselves."

"Max, we don't know if a real relationship will work." I tell him, unsure of even what I'm telling him.

"The relationship that we started was going perfectly, the only problem was that we were in two different cities, but we made it work. And in that time, we got to know one another on a different level, a deeper level and I can absolutely tell you that I've never felt this way about a relationship, a partner before you."

"Max," I say, tears dotting my eyes.

"I love you, Peyton. And I'm not afraid to tell you that I need you too," he says.

I fight the urge to return the sentiment, but is he really here for the right reasons?

Does he love me, or he is just saying what I want him to say?

"Max, I'm not sure this is such a great idea. I don't want you risking everything … on me." I say, clearing my throat.

"What if the x is worth the risk? I've never felt as strongly about a decision as I do right now, live on the edge with me, Pey. This is a chance that sometimes we must take."

"I thought that you don't play the *what ifs* game?"

"This isn't a game. This is an investment in our future as man and wife and for my business."

"But I sent you these," I say holding up the envelope, which I can only assume is the divorce papers that I sent to him.

"And I refuse to sign them." he tells me, his chin raised high and with confidence.

I look at him. He's the same man that I fell in love with, albeit a little tired looking, but I can tell through his posture and his tone that he means business. He's not blowing smoke up my ass and he means every word that he is saying to me.

But what if this is a temporary change.

What if he still wants me to move to Seattle?

Or what if he changes his mind and we don't work out?

MAXWELL

I wait, sitting on her couch, for her to accept my being here. For her to welcome me in and for us to resume our relationship.

Is it that easy though?

Can we resume the relationship that was blossoming before she decided that she couldn't make the move?

Is there something else there that was making her want to stay here in Los Angeles?

"I want us back, I know that we were long-distance and while that's a type of relationship we could have, I want you and I want you every day. I made all the maneuvers to make my home in Los Angeles, and I want my home to be with you."

"But what if we don't work out?"

"But what if we do, Peyton? What if we have the best romance in the history of random hook-ups from Las Vegas? What if we become one of the success stories that authors write about?"

"It's a gamble," she says.

"And I'm all in."

I see the tears in her eyes as I take her hands in mine and move closer to her.

"What if we fizzle out?" she asks.

"Then we at least know that we gave our relationship a real chance."

"Max," she says.

"Peyton," I return.

"I don't know what to say."

"Say that we can make this work?" I plead. "That you will take me back and that I can tear up these papers."

She hesitates, and I can see her emotions warring with her, but she opens her mouth with a small smile and I know that I'm done for.

"So, where would you stay?"

I THOUGHT AHEAD OF TIME, IN CASE SHE DIDN'T WELCOME ME into her home with open arms, and got a vacation rental for the next week and planned to stay there.

"Are you sure about this? I can stay at my place, and we can naturally date this week?" Peyton asks from the inside of the house while I'm checking the BBQ, fiddling with the knobs.

"I'm not going to force you to stay with me, but I would love for you to. It's your call, if it's too much too soon, then just let me know. I'll back off, but I want you to know I'm all in, I'm doing this for us, because I want there to be an us." I reply as I move back inside the house.

"I just don't want to push myself on you," she says.

"I think that it's me, who pushed myself on you. I want you with me, I want you to be involved every inch of the way. I want to run ideas by you and I want you to be a part of my everyday life. I want this."

"I just haven't done anything like this before," she says.

"Neither have I." I say standing in front of her. "I've never gone to these lengths in any relationship before you."

She lays her hand along my cheek and smiles with a tilt of her head.

"I can see how much you are putting yourself out there, and I'm thankful. Please be patient, because this is so sudden. I'm not entirely sure what we're doing, and I think that I need it to sink in a little bit."

"I know, I'm sorry. I don't mean to push, but I just want you to see that I mean business. I am invested, and I want nothing more than anything for this to work. I want us. If you want me to sign the divorce paperwork and we can have no strings tied to our relationship, then I will. I just want to be with you."

"Tell me about this new office that you are opening," she takes my hand and leads me over to the side of the living room where the couch and loveseat is.

Since the company name is widely known, it helps in providing a prominent image that is far greater than a brand new company.

I tell her the gist of what we will continue to do, but the new areas we will see as well as the fact that I will still have travel back and forth between here and Settle as a partner from time to time, but ultimately the intention is to call Los Angeles home.

She nods as I speak and takes in all the information with ease as I give it to her until I tell her the one part that involves her company.

"You mean you want to have my company on reserve for party planning and my name will be in the referral?" she asks.

"That would be my choice, but of course, it's the call of your boss." I tell her.

"I don't plan to go into the actual party planning role of the agency, Max. I enjoy the aspect of managing the office versus the planning aspect. I'm not entirely sure whether or not I want to go into managing projects, or people. That was part of why I turned down Seattle."

"So, I should take your name off of my proposals?" I ask.

"Please? While I enjoyed the planning of that one company's

rebranding, I'm not sure that is the part of the company that I'm suited for," she tells me, with honestly.

"Okay, I can leave you out of it, if that would make you feel comfortable. But can I still have permission to refer our companies to yours?" I question.

"Of course, just leave my name out of it." she says. "I'm sure Mr. Frederick would be thrilled about the referrals."

I nod, "Now, can we stop talking about work, and can I kiss you? I haven't kissed you in weeks, and it's killing me."

She smiles and leans in as I meet her half way and our mouths connect with our tongues in a delicious battle.

CHAPTER TWENTY-ONE

"This one time in Vegas, I gave a small skinny Spiderman a couple dollars for a photo & he tried to lift my fat ass off the ground, he got me a good inch or two!"

PEYTON

It's been an interesting twenty-four hours to say the least. Yesterday, I was minding my own business while decluttering the bookshelves in the living room, and singing along with the movie while I worked as Quinn snored away in her room, when someone knocks on the door.

I wasn't expecting to see Max on my doorstep.

I was expecting a phone call as soon as he received the divorce paperwork, but what I wasn't expecting, was him in the flesh.

He is adamant on not signing the paperwork and just says that he's making a move. A pretty big move, if you ask me.

Am I really worth the risk? The change in his life?

A risk of completely changing his life. Moving from one city to another, for what? For me?

Do I want this?

Absolutely.

But can I ask this of him when, I was not willing to take that risk?

I ignored his calls for a week and told him that I couldn't move. And that was the truth. I was feeling guilt all around, for not talking to my friends about any of what was going on in my life and ultimately about my plans to move out of state, all for what? For a job? Or was it for a guy? The exact same guy who is sleeping in the other room, who is willing to turn his world upside down, because of love. Because of me.

We spent the night together, as if nothing happened. As if I didn't turn him down, and then send him papers to end the accidental marriage. We spent the night wrapped up in one another, making up for the past few weeks.

And now what?

Do we give this another go?

Do I tell him that I can't let him make a massive move like this when there's no guarantee about our future?

"What are you sitting over there lamenting about? Are you second guessing everything?" he asks, breaking me out of my thoughts.

I turn in the direction of his voice, not at all ready for the Adonis who is standing, bare ass naked in the kitchen.

I gulp. "Clothes?"

"On the floor." He shrugs coming up and taking a seat beside me. "I'm going to guess now is not a good time for naked time humor?"

"As much as I enjoy the view, I have to be honest—" I give him a small smile.

"Hold that thought, this moment warrants pants." Max stands, stalks away with his tanned toned ass, almost making me want to ask him to stop.

He returns a few moments later, with gray sweats hanging off his hips, showcasing the delectable vee that I ran my tongue across just hours ago. I lick my lips and shake my head, try to get my thoughts in order as he sits beside me.

"What's on your mind?" he asks.

"Us." I turn my gaze upon him with that single word. I take a deep breath and hold it, waiting for his response.

"Go on?" he pleads.

"I'm scared," I admit. "I'm scared that you're making the wrong choice."

He takes a deep breath and then turns his body fully in towards me as he takes my hands in his.

"Pey," he takes a deep breath. "The only wrong choice that I made, was letting too much time go between when you called me to let me know that you would be staying here."

"Why are you so positive about this? When we don't know what will happen from one day to the next? We don't know what stands in front of us. Whether or not our relationship will last or not. What if you move to LA and we break up?" I ask.

"Then that's just a risk that we will take," he tells me.

"Is it worth it?" I ask.

"Is what worth the risk? Our relationship?"

"The relationship was an accident from the start. We met during a drunken night and don't even remember getting married, or anything that happened. Hell, you didn't even know I existed for months."

"While that may be true, how we started—it doesn't mean that I haven't fallen in love with you along the way. That I'm wanting to take the jump and risk everything for you. I don't know what it is, but I'm not the same guy that I was before you came along.

And I don't want to be. I want to be who I am, when I'm with you."

"So, you want to be a different person?" I ask him confused.

"No, yes, no. I mean, I want to be the person that I am, when I'm with you." He says with a squeeze of my hands. "You make me better. You make me want more than just work in my life."

"But what if—" He releases my hands and places a hand on my cheek.

"We can come up with a shit-ton of 'what ifs' and a lot of scenarios where we wouldn't work out. But we can always come up with a million different ways that we do work out. And that's what I want to focus on, because I want that more than anything."

"Who would have thought that the guy that I end up with is a total sap." I tilt my head and smile.

"Does that mean you'll also take the risk? We'll do this together?" I see the hope in his features as his posture straightens.

"Well, what could it hurt, right?" I say, and before I can finish the sentence, I'm pulled across his lap and his arms engulf me.

"We're going to have so much fun," he whispers against me.

MAXWELL

The week was a mixture of busy, happy and confusing at the same time. The paperwork for the new building was a considerable amount. As well as the next steps of coordinating with my Human Resources team to get the process started.

Within a few days, I was interviewing for the Southern California Human Resources team from a pre-selected pool and had flown down the director of HR along with a few board members to the area.

On the business end, everything was running smooth.

Not the romantic end, it was a mixture of being happy and not getting a hold of how Peyton is feeling about everything. She stayed back at her apartment twice during the week and it left me feeling like she still wasn't sure about us, but when she would return, and she kept her promise about doing so, I couldn't have been happier, clearing up any of the confusion that I was feeling.

But now, I'm back in Seattle, standing in my now empty penthouse and it's all hitting me that this is really happening.

I sold the penthouse. I bought a new house, a modest house, not something that is as extravagant as this place, but a decent sized home in Highland Park. And I packed up my corner at the office.

I'm ready for the new chapter in my life and I think that my mid-thirties are a good time to be able to do whatever the hell I feel like doing, and since it's for love—all the more.

I spent the morning with my sister, planning out for when she can visit, checked in on Scout who is staying with Peyton, and finished with the rest of getting my belongings out of the place.

"Well, it looks like your ass got robbed!" Marcus says from behind me.

I turn around and my best friend and college roommate, Marcus stands with his hands in his front pockets as he looks around the empty space.

"I hope they get some good money for some of the stuff," I reply with a smile as I walk towards him. He's standing in the kitchen and leans back against the counter.

"I can't believe that you're doing this," he shakes his head.

"Doing what? Following my heart?" I ask.

"Becoming such a fucking pussy. I mean Seriously, when did you grow a vagina? Is it shaved or the all-natural type?" He smirks.

"It was only a matter of time. First, you're tied down, and then some of that rubs off on the other guys. Who's next? Jason?" I joke.

"God, that man wouldn't know a good woman, if his life

depended on it. He's too consumed with money and boobs. The more that he can get his hands on, the better."

"Ain't that the truth." I say, and the room goes silent.

For the first time in our friendship, we have an awkward silence.

"So, maybe we can come and visit you? Make a trip and you can show me the sights. I've never been to Los Angeles, you can be my tour guide and shit," he grins.

"Yeah, we can work that out." I tell him slapping the island counter. "So, shall we? We don't wanna keep the rest of the douches waiting on my last night, right?"

"They can wait all they want, this is our special time."

"Are you going to start crying?" I ask.

"Only if you try to hug me, so let's just keep this distance and we'll be good."

"What if I touch your hand, like brush my finger right here." I reach and fuck with him. He pulls his hand back and holds it against his chest.

"One touch may not be enough." He warns pointing at me.

"Let's get out of here, I don't want to hear any bitching," I tell him.

WE WALK INTO THE BAR AND WALK DIRECTLY TO OUR USUAL table. The other guys look up from their conversation as we slide into the circular booth.

"It's about damn time! Were you two making out in the car on the way over here?" Cooper smirks.

"Maxi-pad here was admiring how big his penthouse was for one last time and thinking about how he's going to move into something the size of his kitchen. It was a sad moment, there was consoling and then tears." Marcus jokes.

"Seriously, those homes in LA are probably a lot smaller than anything that you would buy here. What did you get, a shoebox?" Jason asks.

"There's areas with bigger homes, but I figure as long as I'm set with what I need, I won't ask for much else." I shrug.

"He means pussy," Conner laughs, but it's cut short with my elbow into his ribs.

"So, do you have a tight pad? Up in the Hollywood Hills? Maybe Malibu?" Jason asks.

"I bought a four bedroom craftsman house in Highland Park. It's actually really beautiful." I tell them.

"Beautiful? You sound like a total chick. Do you shave your lady bits too? Do you have a landing strip? Maybe a full on bush? Do you and Peyton use a double-edged dildo?" Cooper laughs hysterically.

"I asked him the same thing," Marcus laughs.

At the end of the night, the guys have each taken their respective jabs at me and I let them. We ended the night with a celebratory shot and a round of man-hugs, the type where you don't really hug, but half hug with a hefty pat on the upper shoulder. There may have been grunts and some light sniffles from Marcus, but ultimately, we finished the night on a high and with laughter.

When I walked into the dark and empty penthouse, the weight of the night crashed on my shoulders.

I'm leaving.

I'm leaving the state and starting a whole new life. Perhaps, a new adventure.

And I'm doing part of it, to be with a woman I am one hundred percent in love with.

And my new life starts, tomorrow.

One more sleep.

CHAPTER TWENTY-TWO

"This one time in Vegas, was playing a slot machine at one of the casinos and a guy asked me if I "worked" at the casino."

PEYTON

"You have something on your face," Max leans over and with a brush of his thumb, he wipes the remnants of my condiments from my double-cheese cheeseburger from the corner of my mouth.

Max ordered his burger without the cheese and when the waiter returned with his meal, with cheese on it, Max bit his tongue and as soon as the waiter left, with a death glare at his meal in front of him he started cursing.

At that point, I grabbed his plate and began to scrape the cheese onto my burger, doubling the cheese happily to my burger. It would be a horrible idea to let a perfectly good slice of cheese go to waste.

"I don't understand your issue with cheese on a burger. Cheese is the best on meat. I mean there's so many different variations that you can add and they all have a different taste. Except Bleu cheese, that will never happen. Nope." I pop the "p" and say.

"I like cheese just fine. I just don't like the combination together." He says with a mouthful. "But thank you for doing what is right in the world and putting it on your burger."

"Anytime, I will promise to always take the cheese off of your burgers."

"That's why I think this relationship will work out, just fine," he grins pulling a French fry off his plate and absent-mindedly feeding it to the dog.

"Oh, *that's* why you think it will?" I tease.

"Well, that and the obviousness of how much I'm into you."

He is into me, and I'm into him.

We're in love, and that's not something that I thought would happen.

He moved to Los Angeles a month ago and bought a beautiful craftsman house, which is a bright color of teal, on the top of a small hill you can get to from the street by a cobblestone stairway, or from a driveway on the backside of the property.

I fell in love with his home instantly, from the mahogany framed doorways and windows throughout the house and all the natural light to the wrap around window seat in the den. While I'm still living at my apartment with Quinn, I do spend most of my nights at his house. And slowly, my stuff is landing at his house as well. We haven't discussed officially moving in together, and I'm not entirely sure I want to just assume that's what he wants to do, and so soon. Also, I don't want to leave Quinn in the lurch, but she and I have discussed it, that way, I'm not making the same mistake again, by keeping my friends in the dark.

So, every other night, I sleep over at Max's place and the other nights, Quinn and myself hang out, sometimes with Hanna.

I look over to Max and smile, wishing that we could stay in this spot forever and bottle up our moment. Happy, healthy and with full tummies.

"I've got to head back to the office, but I'll see you later tonight?" I ask standing.

"Of course, I have an afternoon full of meetings and interviews. Care to pick up dinner on your way over? I still need to get the hang of grocery shopping or delivery." He stands up and wraps an arm around my waist to pull me close to him as he kisses my temple. I smile and lean into the kiss.

Yeah. I would bottle up this moment in an instant.

MAXWELL

My nerves are at a record level high, and I'm not even sure that I'm breathing properly. I'm sure that I've forgotten a few things in the transition between Seattle and Los Angeles, but I have an amazing group of staff who have worked hard the past month to get this location up and running.

Today is officially the first day that we have all staff on board and our doors are open, figuratively. And once I'm finished with the first official business day, I have a full room to decorate to ask Peyton an important question.

But first, the day must begin.

We start with a full company meeting, we announce all key managers and break out in groups for team building activities. The day flies quickly, and I see plenty of happy smiling faces while I walk around. I did what I could to make myself available, to listen with intent and to be an interactive leader since I was virtually a stranger to all of them.

After lunch, we have more discussions, then I release everyone early.

Once I'm home, I walk into the second bedroom that I haven't started to fill up with furniture and begin opening the boxes and displaying the contents evenly around the room.

I finish in record time and stand back from the doorway and look at everything that I've done. Calendars and planners line every inch of the bedroom, including the ceiling. I know that Peyton is obsessed with Calendars and hope that she will not only be shocked when I bring her up here after we eat dinner, but will no doubt say yes to me.

"You outdid yourself with dinner tonight. Have you been watching YouTube on how to cook?" Peyton jokes placing her silverware on her plate and sits back in her chair.

"I may have had a little assistance in the kitchen. I found this awesome app that shows you step by step how to do it. There was a lot of pausing and rewinding, but I'm glad you liked it." I smile and stand while leaning over to pick up her plate and mine to take into the kitchen.

"Well, I salute you. It was delicious. Hey, do you mind if I run a load of laundry? I forgot to take home some of my dirty clothes the other night."

I place the plates in the sink and turn to her, my hands behind my back and placed on the edge of the counter.

She's given me the perfect prompt. *Let's do this. It's time.*

"I've got something that I want to show you," I tell her, regulating my breathing to remain calm.

"Did you find a new special room in the house?" She laughs as I did find a door that was covered to a basement in the kitchen.

Which is strange, because there aren't many basements in California.

"Just wait, come with me." I hold my hand out to her and lead her around the corner and up the stairs.

"Okay, are you ready?" I turn and look at her.

"What's going on, Max, you're acting weird. Did you finally add a bed and stuff in here? Wanna share your manly decoration skills or something."

"Close your eyes," I say and with a pout, she does. I take her hand again in mine and bring her into the center of the room slowly. "Okay, keep them closed."

I turn on the light and then return to stand in front of her and take a deep breath.

I look around the room once more and then tell her to open her eyes.

My hands are still gripping onto hers and I'm watching the wheels in her head spin as she takes in the room. I release her hands as she begins to turn in place.

"What's all this?" she asks as Scout comes into the room, sniffing around the edges around the spare bedroom.

"I know that you have a thing for all things calendars and I thought it would be a memorable way to ask you something."

She places a hand on her hips and looks at me. "Should I be more nervous than I am right now?"

"No, not at all. Okay, so this is something I've wanted to do since moving to Los Angeles, and I couldn't think of a better way to make it something that you will remember," I smile, prolonging asking her.

After a few seconds of silence, she rolls her eyes.

"Okay, the suspense is killing me." She bounces on the tips of her toes in anticipation.

"Will you move in with me?"

EPILOGUE

"This one time in Vegas, I accidentally got married."

THREE YEARS **Later**

"I now pronounce you, husband and wife, you may now kiss the bride," the priest says.

I lean forward at the same time that Max does, and we meet in the middle. Our joined hands wrap around one another for a brief moment and then we pull apart, not wanting to gross everyone out with a full on make-out session like we did last night at the rehearsal dinner.

We invited thirty people, and each one of them stand up and clap as we turn to face them. With our hands up in the air, there is barking from Scout in combination with hoots and hollers while we walk down the aisle past our guests.

We held our wedding in our backyard in the late afternoon. There were string lights hanging above the entire space, and "L" shape table along the edges of the property for our dinner. We had white flowers throughout the space, to stand out amongst the teal of the house and the green of the grass. The setting couldn't be more perfect, and yet today—it is.

We made it.

Even though our wedding was legal in Vegas three years ago, only our closest friends knew about it. I knew that Max's mom and sister wouldn't be too pleased if we told them we got married when I first met them when Max flew them both out to LA for Thanksgiving. So, we kept the fact that we were already married to ourselves and our friend group, but got re-married on the exact same day that we did before.

That was Max's brilliant idea. I'm pretty sure that it was a way that he would be able to play it safe with only having to remember one anniversary date. I mean, it is the day we met, our first date and the day we got married twice all in one date.

Standing in a circle with Max's friends and mine with a shot glass in our hands as we wait for Marcus to give his little speech.

"I knew from the moment that this man mentioned he was married that it wasn't a mistake, but a blessing. Max turned from the workaholic to the guy who realized that he was missing out, and I thank you, Peyton for being the drunk girl dancing on a table in the VIP section to help him realize what he's been missing the whole time. To Peyton and Max!" Marcus smiles.

We all hold the shot glasses up then take our shots.

"My turn! My turn!" Quinn says excitedly.

"Another round of shots!" Jason says, turning and holding up his hand to the bartender behind us, stationed against the house.

He turns around with a drink platter a moment later and smiles as he gives us all a shot.

"I want to thank you, Max, for moving here to Los Angeles. For giving our girl here the best love of her life and then letting us actually come to the party this time! Cheers to the official married couple!" She holds up her shot glass and then we all take our shots.

"Okay, no more shots. I want to be able to properly walk by the end of the night, and not have my wedding be another black-out." Max waves his hand as Jason looks like he was going to go next.

Jason pouts playfully and Max shakes his head.

"Hey Jason, why don't we go and tear up that dance floor? I need to dance, and I'm pretty sure you're going to be my partner in crime tonight," Quinn steps forward and holds out her hand to him. He looks at it, smiles and then takes it.

"See ya suckers!" he says trailing behind my best friend.

After that, our group disperses, leaving Max and myself alone.

"Hey, I can finally call you Mrs. Addison outside of the house. I can call you wifey, and out of any of those other things, Mrs. Addison is and will always be my favorite though." Max smiles as he steps closer to me and wraps his arm around my waist as we stand side by side watching the small crowd gathered in our backyard while music plays from our outdoor sound system and people dance here and there.

"That's true, Mr. Addison." I lean my head against his shoulder.

"You know, after Marcus's wedding, the guys and I were sitting around, playing poker, shooting the shit and drinking. We were talking about marriage and trying to not be super poetic. But I remember vaguely saying something about the length of time, and when you know, you know."

"Oh yeah?" I look up at him. "And what would that amazing bit of knowledge be?"

"I said something like, when I find my someone, I'll be a goner. And my darling wife, from the moment that I re-met you, I was yours. I was definitely a goner." He leans down and kisses the tip of my nose.

"You were pretty smitten with me," I tease.

"Even when you tried to divorce me, I knew I wouldn't let you go." He turns and faces me, both his hands sliding around my waist.

"I don't know what I did right to deserve you," I whisper as his lips meet mine for a gentle kiss.

"I'll tell you what you did, you apparently talked me into marrying you, then made me fall in love with you and your crazy witchcrafty ways, then got me to marry you all over again." He smirks.

I hear the clinking of several forks against glass and smile.

"Mr. Addison, they want us to kiss," I tell him.

"Well, I wouldn't want to disappoint our adoring fans."

And we didn't.

ACKNOWLEDGMENTS

Where do I begin with this?

I think that writing this book was one of my most favorite experiences, because I got to include some of the readers in a small way.

Thank you, the readers number one for reading!

Thank you to my tribe, Jess, Maren, Shay & Mary for in one way or another supporting me.

Thank you to my husband, who didn't complain as I spent my weekends writing, and laughed with me at some of my ideas.

DEAR FRIENDS,

Thank you so much for your support. If you enjoyed this book, please sign up for my newsletters so you can be in the know when a new book comes out, or if you just want to hear me ramble about nonsense.

My newsletter has sneak peeks of upcoming books, giveaways, and also fun stuff. SIGN UP HERE

Please check out my website at: WWW. TARRAHANDERS.COM

I hope that in some shape or form you felt connected to my characters, I strive to have my stories be as relatable as possible, and not too outrageous. The sole purpose for me to bring my friends these stories is to feel like that too can be you.

That being said, I write to make you happy. I wouldn't be able to do so without your feedback. Whether if you leave a review on your favorite book retail site (Please do that would be spectacular) or if you feel like shooting me a message at: tarrah.anders@gmail.com . I would love to hear from you.

All my best,
Smooches ~ Tarrah

xo ♥ xo
Tarrah Anders

READ MORE BY TARRAH

THE NEIGHBORHOOD SERIES

THE MELTED SERIES

THE NIGHT MOVES SERIES

WHAT HAPPENS IN… SERIES

STANDALONES

New Year, New You

The Brute

Summer Fling

CLUTCH Endgame

Change of Scenery

More than Friends

No More Heartache

Fly Girl

Speakeasy (Storybook Pub Anthology)

In the End (A Quarantine Romance)

Rookie Moves (A Quick Snap Novella)

Love Surreptitiously

Little White Lie

Love on the Sidelines (A Quick Snap Novella)

Heartburn (An Everyday Heroes World Novel)

Do you want more info about Tarrah Anders and her releases? Sign up for her <u>VIP Newsletter</u> today!

Tarrah Anders is a contemporary romance author who is all about the feels, with the twists of sexy mixed in between. Writing has always been a passion and Tarrah loves to share her words, her characters and the world that they live in with her readers. Tarrah enjoys creating characters that you can be friends with, so get ready to make some new friends.

She is originally from the San Francisco Bay Area, but living in beautiful San Diego with her family, while working in Program Management within the social work field.

Printed in Great Britain
by Amazon